Benziger Brothers

The hymn-book of The new Sunday-school companion

Being the melodies and accompaniments of the mass vespers, and hymns

Benziger Brothers

The hymn-book of The new Sunday-school companion
Being the melodies and accompaniments of the mass vespers, and hymns

ISBN/EAN: 9783741197635

Manufactured in Europe, USA, Canada, Australia, Japa

Cover: Foto ©Andreas Hilbeck / pixelio.de

Manufactured and distributed by brebook publishing software
(www.brebook.com)

Benziger Brothers

The hymn-book of The new Sunday-school companion

THE

Hymn-Book

OF

The New Sunday-School Companion.

BEING

THE MELODIES AND ACCOMPANIMENTS

OF

THE MASS, VESPERS, AND HYMNS

CONTAINED IN

"THE NEW SUNDAY-SCHOOL COMPANION."

SECOND EDITION.

NEW YORK, CINCINNATI, CHICAGO:

BENZIGER BROTHERS,

Printers to the Holy Apostolic See.

Imprimatur.

✠ MICHAEL AUGUSTINE,

Archbishop of New York.

NEW YORK, *September* 19, 1889.

APPROBATIONS.

Rt. Rev. L. de Goesbriand, D.D., Bishop of Burlington, Vt.: "I consider the selection of the melodious airs for the English hymns and the few Latin pieces contained in the COMPANION a very judicious one. I consider the SUNDAY-SCHOOL COMPANION and the music for its hymns the most useful publication that we possess for the use of catechism classes and of their teachers."

Rt. Rev. Tobias Mullen, D.D., Bishop of Erie, Pa.: "A very opportune publication, and will prove very serviceable not only in the Sunday-school, but in all churches where a special Mass is celebrated on days of obligation for the exclusive convenience of children."

Rev. Aloys T. Brucker, S.J., Conejos, Col.: "Supplies a real want. I had anxiously wished, for some time, to see the music of the last part of the COMPANION, especially for my Sunday-school children. For all practical purposes it is complete and varied."

Rev. J. J. Dougherty, D.D., St. Monica's Church, New York: "I gladly recommend the HYMN-BOOK OF THE NEW SUNDAY-SCHOOL COMPANION as a concise and comprehensive CHOIR-MANUAL. . . . I have introduced the book into my school, and am well satisfied with it."

Rev. M. J. Phelan, St. Cecilia's Church, New York: "Answers all our purposes. . . . It only needs examination to have it adopted, and I must say it is the Manual we have been looking for."

Rev. T. J. O'Reilly, St. Dominic's Church, Columbus, O.: "I have introduced your HYMN-BOOK into my Sunday-school, and am pleased to state that I appreciate its worth very highly."

Rev. P. McNamara, Toronto, Iowa: "I am very much pleased with the HYMN-BOOK. Our choir have been using it with more success than large and costly choir-books. I think it is just the book for country choirs."

Rev. James Coyne, Lanesboro, Minn.: "Your new HYMN-BOOK OF THE NEW SUNDAY-SCHOOL COMPANION has taken very well here. It is just the thing wanted. Its marvellous cheapness and its handiness, no less than the judicious selection of music and words, will do a great deal towards the increase of Catholic church music among the people."

PREFACE.

———————●———————

At the earnest request of many who are using *The New Sunday-School Companion*, the publishers have been induced to issue this music book as a complement to that excellent and popular little book.

In choosing the material, great care has been taken to select only such music as is good and suitable for church use, avoiding everything of a light or frivolous character.

The GREGORIAN REQUIEM MASS with ACCOMPANIMENT has been introduced, although not in the NEW SUNDAY-SCHOOL COMPANION, as it has been thought a necessity for the completeness of the book.

The arrangement is in an easy and simple style throughout, although presenting no little variety, and is within the capacity of any piano player of moderate ability.

Although this Hymn-book was chiefly made as a supplement to *The New Sunday-School Companion*, it is, nevertheless, *complete in itself*, and will well serve as a CHOIR-MANUAL FOR SCHOOLS, SODALITIES, or COUNTRY CHURCHES.

Wherever *The New Sunday-School Companion* is introduced, it will be found of great advantage to provide the best singers (if not all the singers) with copies of this music book. The singing of the whole congregation will thus be properly led, and the organist's task be greatly lightened.

The publishers beg leave to return their acknowledgments to all to whom they are indebted for kind assistance and suggestions, as well as to those who, by their kind permission, have enabled them to use much valuable material.

CONTENTS.

CLASSIFICATION OF HYMNS.

Unison Mass.*

*The top line of notes is the **Melody**, and only this is to be sung.* The chords are for instrumental—Piano or Organ—accompaniment.

The Solo parts may be sung by one or a few select voices. In the Chorus parts all the voices join.

The director of the choir should insist on the observance of the different marks of expression, *piano, forte, lento*, etc., and confine the singers to a strict unison throughout.

KYRIE.

---

* Taken, by permission, from the "Manual of Select Catholic Hymns and Devotions for the use of Schools, Colleges, Academies, and Congregations." Compiled and arranged from Approved Sources by Rev. P. M. Colonel, C. SS. R.

5

GLORIA.

ca - mus te. Gra - ti - as a - gi - mus ti - bi prop - ter magnam

glo - ri - am tu - - am. Do - mi - ne De - us, Rex cœ - le - stis,

De - us, Pa - - ter om - ni - po - tens. Do - mi - ne

Fi - li u - ni ge - ni - te. Je - - su Chri - ste.

Do - mi-ne De - us, A - gnus De - i, Fi - li-us Pa - tris.

Qui tol-lis pec - ca - - - - ta mun - - - di, mi - se -

re - - - - - re no - - - bis. Qui tol - -

- - lis pec - ca - ta mun - - di, su - sci-pe de-pre-ca - ti - o - nem

no - - stram. Qui se - des ad dex - te - ram Pa - - - tris,

. mi - se - re - re no - - - - bis. Quo - ni - am tu so - lus sanc -

tus, Tu so - lus Do - mi - nus. Tu so - lus Al - tis - si - mus,

Je - su Chri - ste. Cum sanc - to Spi - ri - tu in glo - ri - a

De - i Pa - - -tris. A - - - - - - - men.

UNISONO.

℣. Dominus vobiscum.   ℟. Et cum Spi - ri - tu tu - o.

℣. Oremus. . . .
per omnia sæcula
sæculorum.   ℟. A - men.

After the
Epistle: ℟. De - o gra - ti - as.

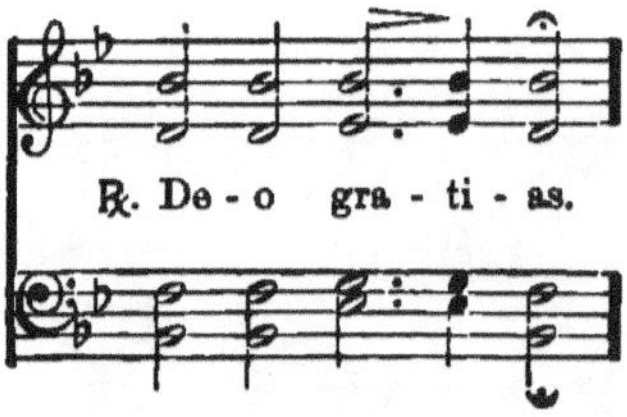

℣. Dominus vobiscum.   ℟. Et cum spiritu tuo.

℣. Sequentia
sancti Evangelii
secundum Mat-
thæum.   ℟. Gloria ti-bi Domi - ne.

After
the
Gospel: ℟. Laus ti - bi Chri-ste.

CREDO.

Pa - trem om - ni - po - ten-tem, fac - to - rem cœ - li et ter - -

ræ, vi - si - bi - li-um om - ni - um, et in - vi - si - bi - li-um.

Et in u - num Do - mi-num Je - sum Chri - stum, Fi - li-um

De - i u - ni - ge - ni - tum. Et.... ex Pa - tre na - tum

Qui prop - ter nos ho - mi-nes, et propter nostram sa-lu - - tem de-

scen-dit de cœ - - - lis. Et in-car - na-tus est de Spi - ri - tu

Sanc - to ex Ma-ri - a vir - gi - ne, ET HO - MO FA - CTUS EST.

Cru - ci - fi - xus e - ti-am pro no - - - bis sub Pon - ti-o Pi-

la - to,   pas - sus, et se - pul - - - tus est.

f Chorus.

Spiritoso.

Et re - sur - re - xit ter - - - ti - a di - e   se - cun-dum scrip-

tu - ras,   et a - scen-dit in cœ - lum,   se - det ad

mp Solo.

dex - te - ram Pa - - tris. Et i - te-rum ven - tu-rus est cum

glo - ri - a ju - di - ca - re vi - vos, et mor - tu - os,

f CHORUS.   *mp* SOLO.

Cu - jus re - gni non e - rit fi - nis. Et in Spi-ri-tum

san - ctum Do - mi - num, et vi - vi - fi - can - tem, qui ex

f CHORUS.

Pa - tre Fi - li - o - que pro - ce - dit. Qui cum Pa - tre et

Fi - li - o si - mul a - do - ra - tur et con - glo - ri - fi -

ca - tur, qui lo - cu - tus est per Pro - phe - - - tas.

mp Solo.

Et u - nam, San - ctam Ca - tho - li - cam, et A - po -

f Chorus.

sto - li - cam Ec - cle - si - am. Con - fi - te - or u - num Bap -

tis - - ma in re - mis - si - o - nem pec - ca - to - - rum.

mp Solo.

Et ex - pe - cto re - sur - re - cti - o - nem mor - tu - o - - rum.

f Chorus.

Et vi - - tam ven - tu - ri sæ - - - - cu -

li. A - - - - - - - - - men.

℣. Dominus vobiscum.   ℞. Et cum spiritu tuo.   ℣. Oremus.

During the OFFERTORY a short *latin* hymn to the Blessed Sacrament or to the B. V. Mary may be sung.

RESPONSES AT PREFACE.

℣. Per omnia
    sæcula
    sæculorum.   ℞. A - men.   ℣. Dominus
                                            vobiscum.   ℞. Et cum spi - ri - tu tu - o.

℣. Sursum Corda.   ℞. Ha - be - - - mus ad Do - - mi - num.

℣. Gratias agamus,
    etc.   ℞. Di - - - gnum et ju - - - stum est.

SANCTUS.

ter - ra glo - ri - a tu - - - a. Ho - san - - -

- - na in ex - cel - - - - - - - - sis.

BENEDICTUS.

p Solo.

Be - ne - di - - - ctus qui ve - nit in no - -

- mi - ne Do - - - mi - ni. Ho - san - -

- - na in ex - cel - - - - - - - tis.

AT THE PATER NOSTER.

℣. Per omnia saecula saeculorum.

℟. A - men.

℣. . . . . et ne nos inducas in tentationem.

℟. Sed li - be-ra nos a ma - lo.

℣. Per omnia saecula saeculorum.

℟. A - men.

℣. Pax Domini sit semper vobiscum.

℟. Et cum spi-ri-tu tu - o.

AGNUS DEI.

Chorus.
p Andante devoto.

A - gnus De - i, qui tol - lis pec - ca - ta mun - di,

mi - se - re - re no - - - - bis. A-gnus De - i,   qui tol -

lis pec - ca - ta mun - di,   mi - se - re - - re no - bis.

A - gnus De - - i,   qui tol - - lis pec - ca - ta mun - -

di,   do - - - - - na no - bis pa - - cem.

℣. Dominus vobiscum.   ℞. Et cum spiritu tuo.

℣. Oremus........Per omnia sæcula sæculorum.   ℞. Amen.

℣. Dominus vobiscum.   ℞. Et cum spiritu tuo.

EASTER TIME.

I - te mi - ssa est al - le - lu - ja, al - le - - -

℞. De - o gra - ti - as al - le - lu - ja, al - le - - -

lu - - ja............   **SOLEMN.**   I - - - - -

lu - - ja............   De - - - - -

- - te, e...............   e...............................

- - o. o...............   o...............

e...............   e.....................   mi - ssa est.

o...............   o.....................   gra - ti - as.

DUPLEX.

Ite.. e........................
Deo.. o........................

e.. e mi - ssa est.
o.. o gra - ti - as.

B. V. M.

I - - - te   e.................... mi - ssa est.
De - - - o   o.................... gra - ti - as.

EPISCOPAL BENEDICTION.

℣. Sit nomen Domini bene-dictum.   ℟. Ex hoc nunc et
                                            usque in.... sæ-cu-lum.

℣. Adjutorium nostrum
     in nomine .... Domini.   ℟. Qui fecit cœlum et ter - ram.
℣. Benedicat vos, etc.   ℟. A - men.

Vespers for Sundays.

(See "The New Sunday School Companion," page 126.)

For the convenience of both Organist and Choir we give here, in addition to that in the New Sunday School Companion, the complete Vespers in easy style, with the Tones of the Psalms simplified, so that they can be easily learned by heart by the singers. With the aid of the New Sunday School Companion, wherein all the different Tones are be to found on page 196, etc., the Organist can make any desirable change without difficulty.

PRIEST.

De-us, in ad-ju-tó - rium meum in - tén - de.

CHORUS.

Dómine ad adjuván -
Glória Patri et Filio |

dum me........ fes - tí - na.
et Spirítui.. ..... San-cto.

Sicut erat in princípio | et nunc et semper |

{ N. B.—From Septuagesima till Holy Thursday, no
Alleluja, but the following :—

et in sæcula
sæculórum. | A-men. Al-le-lu-ja. Laus tibi Dómine, Rex ætérnæ glo-ri-æ.

DIXIT DOMINUS.   Psalm 109.   ☞

1. Dixit Dominus, Dómino.......................... me - o ;

2. Donec ponam, inimícos .... tu - os,
3. Virgam virtútis tuæ, emittet Dominus ex .... Si - on,
4. Técum princípium in die virtútis tuæ, in splendóri-
     bus sanc - - - - - - - - - - - - tó - rum,
5. Jurávit Dominus, et non pœnitébit .... e - um,
6. Dominus a dextris................................... tu - is,
7. Judicábit in natiónibus, implébit .... rú - inas,
8. De torrénte, in via................................. bi - bet,
9. Gloria Patri, et .... Fi - lio,
10. Sicut érat in princípio, et nunc, et.................. sem - per,

CONFITEBOR.   Psalm 110.   ☞

1. Confitébor tibi Dómine, in toto .... cor - de   me - o,

2. Magna .... ó - pera   Domini;
3. Conféssio, et magnificéntia .... o - pus   e - jus;
4. Memóriam fécit mirabílium suórum, miséricors
     et mise - - - - - - - - rá - tor   Dominus;
5. Mémor érit in sæculum, testa - - - - mén - ti   su - i;
6. Ut det illis, hæredi - - - - - tá - tem   géntium;
7. Fidélia omnia mandáta ejus, confirmáta in.... sáe - culum   sáe - culi;
8. Redemptiónem misit .... pó - pulo   su - o;
9. Sanctum et terríbile......................... nó - men   e - jus;
10. Intelléctus bónus ómnibus, faci - - - én - tibus   e - um;
11. Gloria...................................... Patri, et   Fi - lio;
12. Sicut erat in princípio, et................... nunc, et   sem - per;

DIXIT DOMINUS. Concluded.

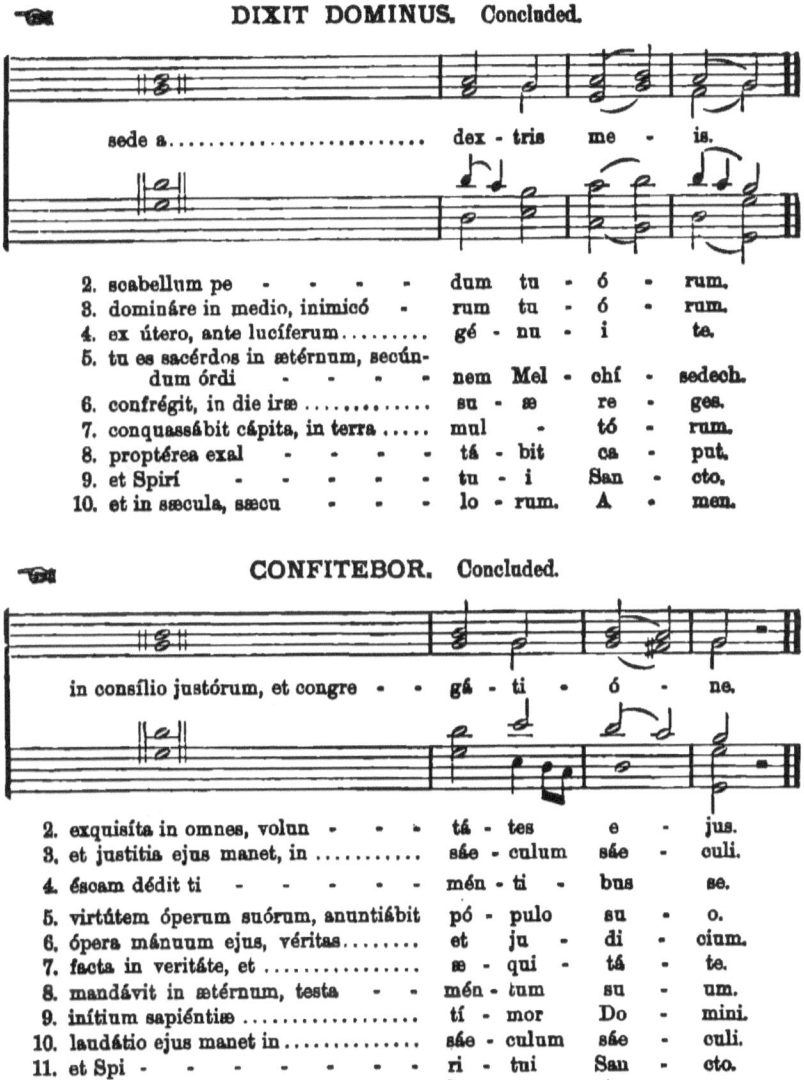

sede a.......................... dex - tris   me - is.

2. scabellum pe - - - - dum   tu - ó - rum.
3. dominâre in medio, inimicó - rum   tu - ó - rum.
4. ex útero, ante lucíferum......... gé - nu - i   te.
5. tu es sacérdos in ætérnum, secún-
      dum órdi - - - - nem Mel - chí - sedech.
6. confrégit, in die iræ............. su - æ   re - ges.
7. conquassábit cápita, in terra..... mul - tó - rum.
8. proptérea exal - - - - tá - bit ca - put.
9. et Spirí - - - - - tu - i   San - cto,
10. et in sæcula, sæcu - - - lo - rum. A - men.

CONFITEBOR. Concluded.

in consílio justórum, et congre - - gá - ti - ó - ne.

2. exquisíta in omnes, volun - - - tá - tes   e - jus.
3. et justitia ejus manet, in........... sǽe - culum sǽe - culi.
4. éscam dédit ti - - - - - mén - ti - bus   se.
5. virtútem óperum suórum, anuntiábit pó - pulo su - o.
6. ópera mánuum ejus, véritas........ et ju - di - cium.
7. facta in veritáte, et............... æ - qui - tá - te.
8. mandávit in ætérnum, testa - - mén - tum su - um.
9. inítium sapiéntiæ.................. tí - mor   Do - mini.
10. laudátio ejus manet in............. sǽe - culum sǽe - culi.
11. et Spi - - - - - - - ri - tui   San - cto.
12. et in sæcula, sæcu - - - - lo - rum. A - men.

BEATUS VIR. Psalm 111.

1. Beátus vir, qui..............................   ti - met   Dóminum;

2. Potens in terra erit.........................   se - men   e - jus;
3. Gloria et divítiæ in ....   do - mo   e - jus;
4. Exórtum est in ténebris ....   lu - men   re - ctis;
5. Jucúndus homo qui miserétur, et commodát|
   dispónet sermónes súos ....   in   ju - dí - cio;
6. In memória ætérna ....   e - rit   ju - stus;
7. Parátum cor ejus speráre in Dómino | confir-
   mátum.................................   est cor   e - jus;
8. Dispérsit dedit paupéribus, justítia ejus mánet in sáe - culum sáe - culi;
9. Peccátor vidébit et irascétur, déntibus suis
   fremet ....   et   ta - bé - scet;
10. Gloria ....   Patri, et   Fi - lio;
11. Sicut erat in princípio, et................... nunc et   sem - per;

LAUDATE PUERI. Psalm 112.

1. Laudáte púeri ....   Dóminum;

2. Sit nomen Domini bene - - - - - - - -   dí - ctum;
3. A solis órtu usque ad oc - - - - - - -   cá - sum;
4. Excélsus super omnes Gentes ....   Dominus;
5. Quis sicut Dóminus Deus noster, qui in altis ....   há - bitat;
6. Súscitans, a terra..   ín - opem;
7. Ut cóllocet eum cum prin - - - - - - -   cí - pibus;
8. Qui habitáre facit stérilem in............................... do - mo;
9. Gloria Patri, et ....   Fi - lio;
10. Sicut érat in princípio, et nunc et .... sem - per;

BEATUS VIR. Concluded.

in mandátis ejus.................... vo - let   ni - mis.

2. generátio rectórum	be	- nedi -	cé	-	tur.
3. et justitia ejus manet, in	sáe.	- culum	sáe	-	culi.
4. miséricors et mise - - - -	rá	- tor et	ju	-	stus.
5. quía in ætérnum non	com	- mo -	vé	-	bitur.
6. ab auditióne mála	non	ti -	mé	-	bit.
7. non commovébitur dónec despíciat ini - - - - - -	mí	- cos	su	-	os.
8. córnu ejus exaltábi - - - -	tur	iu	glo	-	ria.
9. desidérium pecca - - - -	tó	- rum	perí	-	bit.
10. et Spi - - - - - - -	rí	- tui	San	-	cto.
11. et in sæcula sæcu - - - -	lo	- rum.	A	-	men.

LAUDATE PUERI. Concluded.

Laudáte........................ no - men   Do - mi - ni.

2. ex hoc nunc, et.....................	úsque	in	sæ	- cu -	lum.
3. laudábile	no	- men	Do	- mi -	ni.
4. et super cœlos	glo	- ria	e	- -	jus.
5. et humília réspicit, in cœlo	et	in	ter	- -	ra?
6. et de stércore.....................	éri	- gens	paú	- pe -	rem.
7. cum princípibus	pó	- puli	su	- -	i.
8. matrem filió - - - - -	rum	læ -	tan	- -	tem.
9. et Spirí - - - - - -	tu	- i	San	- -	cto.
10. et in sæcula sæcu - - - -	lo	- rum.	A	- -	men.

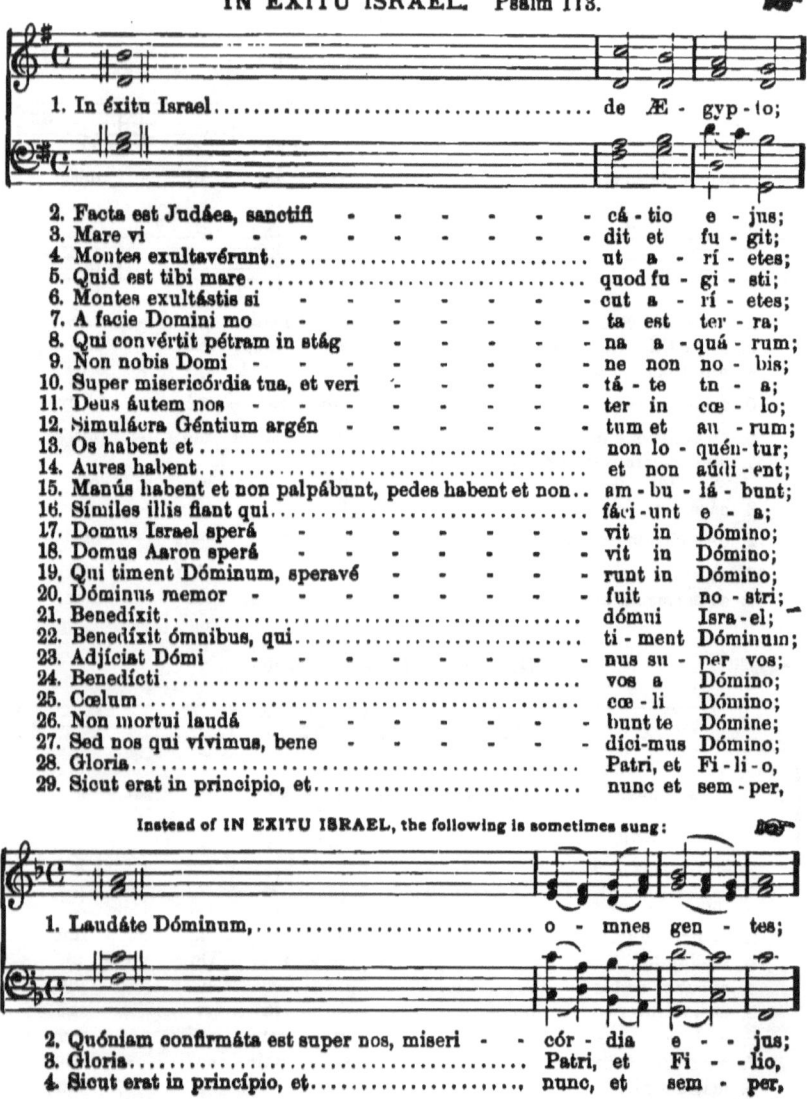

1. In éxitu Israel.. de Æ - gyp - to;

2. Facta est Judǽa, sanctifi - - - - - - - cá - tio e - jus;
3. Mare vi - - - - - - - - dit et fu - git;
4. Montes exultavérunt.................................. ut a - rí - etes;
5. Quid est tibi mare................................... quod fu - gi - sti;
6. Montes exultástis si - - - - - - - - cut a - rí - etes;
7. A facie Domini mo - - - - - - - - ta est ter - ra;
8. Qui convértit pétram in stág - - - - - - na a - quá - rum;
9. Non nobis Domi - - - - - - - ne non no - bis;
10. Super misericórdia tua, et veri - - - - - - tá - te tu - a;
11. Deus áutem nos - - - - - - - - ter in cœ - lo;
12. Simulácra Géntium argén - - - - - - tum et au - rum;
13. Os habent et... non lo - quén - tur;
14. Aures habent.. et non aúdi - ent;
15. Manús habent et non palpábunt, pedes habent et non.. am - bu - lá - bunt;
16. Símiles illis fiant qui................................. fáci - unt e - a;
17. Domus Israel sperá - - - - - - - vit in Dómino;
18. Domus Aaron sperá - - - - - - - vit in Dómino;
19. Qui timent Dóminum, speravé - - - - runt in Dómino;
20. Dóminus memor - - - - - - - - fuit no - stri;
21. Benedíxit... dómui Isra - el;
22. Benedíxit ómnibus, qui.............................. ti - ment Dóminum;
23. Adjíciat Dómi - - - - - - - - nus su - per vos;
24. Benedícti... vos a Dómino;
25. Cœlum.. cœ - li Dómino;
26. Non mortui laudá - - - - - - - bunt te Dómine;
27. Sed nos qui vívimus, bene - - - - - - díci - mus Dómino;
28. Gloria.. Patri, et Fi - li - o,
29. Sicut erat in principio, et.......................... nunc et sem - per,

Instead of IN EXITU ISRAEL, the following is sometimes sung:

1. Laudáte Dóminum,.............................. o - mnes gen - tes;

2. Quóniam confirmáta est super nos, miseri - - cór - dia e - jus;
3. Gloria... Patri, et Fi - lio,
4. Sicut erat in princípio, et.......................... nunc, et sem - per,

IN EXITU ISRAEL. Concluded.

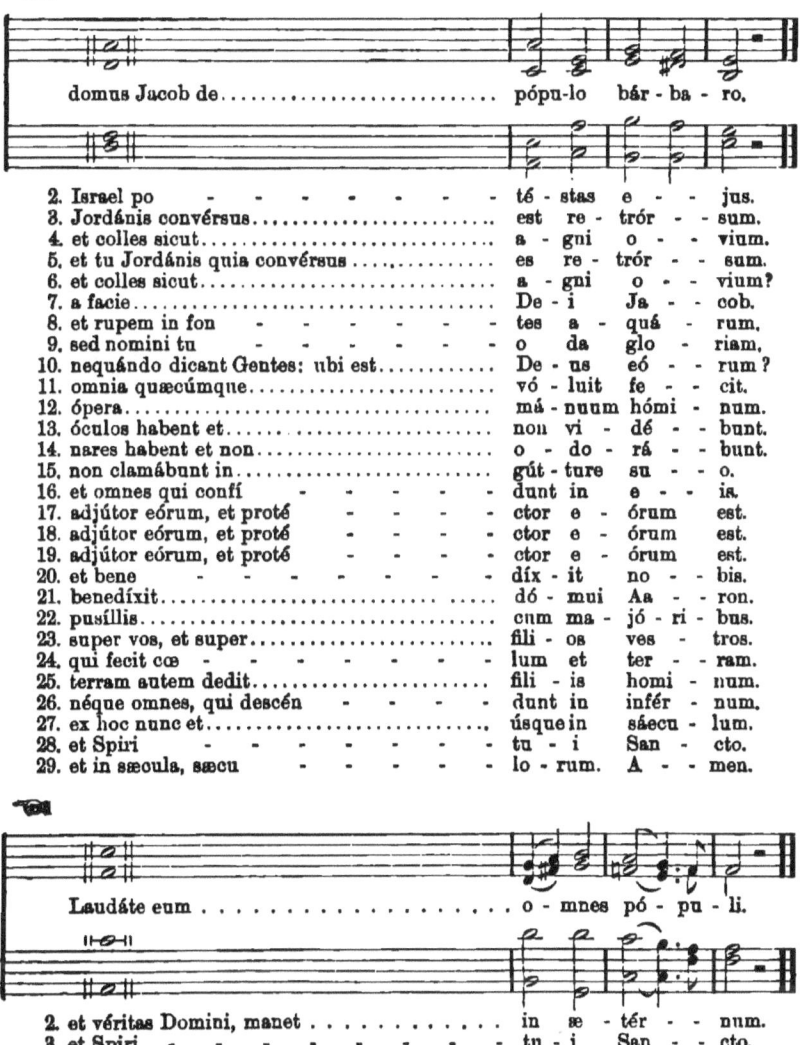

domus Jacob de.......................... pópu-lo bár - ba - ro.

2. Israel po - - - - - - té - stas e - - jus.
3. Jordánis convérsus........................ est re - trór - - sum.
4. et colles sicut............................. a - gni o - - vium.
5. et tu Jordánis quia convérsus .... es re - trór - - sum.
6. et colles sicut............................ a - gni o - - vium?
7. a facie.................................... De - i Ja - - cob.
8. et rupem in fon - - - - - - tes a - quá - rum.
9. sed nomini tu - - - - - - o da glo - riam.
10. nequándo dicant Gentes: ubi est........... De - us eó - - rum?
11. omnia quæcúmque........................ vó - luit fe - - cit.
12. ópera...................................... má - nuum hómi - num.
13. óculos habent et.......... .... non vi - dé - - bunt.
14. nares habent et non...................... o - do - rá - - bunt.
15. non clamábunt in...................... gút - ture su - - o.
16. et omnes qui confí - - - - - dunt in e - - is.
17. adjútor eórum, et proté - - - - ctor e - órum est.
18. adjútor eórum, et proté - - - - ctor e - órum est.
19. adjútor eórum, et proté - - - - ctor e - órum est.
20. et bene - - - - - - - díx - it no - - bis.
21. benedíxit.............................. ..... dó - mui Aa - - ron.
22. pusíllis.................................. cum ma - jó - ri - bus.
23. super vos, et super...................... fili - os ves - tros.
24. qui fecit cœ - - - - - - - lum et ter - - ram.
25. terram autem dedit...................... fili - is homi - num.
26. néque omnes, qui descén - - - - dunt in inférr - num.
27. ex hoc nunc et........................, úsque in sáecu - lum.
28. et Spiri - - - - - - - tu - i San - cto.
29. et in sæcula, sæcu - - - - - lo - rum. A - - men.

Laudáte eum .... o - mnes pó - pu - li.

2. et véritas Domini, manet .... in æ - tér - - num.
3. et Spiri - - - - - - - - tu - i San - - cto.
4. et in sæcula, sæcu - - - - - lo - rum. A - - men.

After the Priest has read the "LITTLE CHAPTER," the Choir responds :

℟. De - o grá - ti - as.

LUCIS CREATOR.

1. Lu - cis Cre - á - tor ó - pti - me, Lu - cem di - é - rum pró - fe - rens,
2. Qui ma - ne junctum vés - pe - ri Di - em vo - ca - ri prǽ - ci - pis,

Pri - mór - di - is lu - cis no - væ, Mun-di pa-rans o - rí-gi-nem.
Il - lá - bi - tur te - trum chaos, Au - di pre-ces cum flé-ti - bus. A-men.

3. Ne mens grávata crímine,
   Vitæ sit exul múnere,
   Dum nil perénne cógitat,
   Seséque culpis ílligat.

4. Cœléste pulset óstium:
   Vitále tollat práemium;

Vitémus omne noxium:
Purgémus omne péssimum.

5. Præsta, pater piíssime,
   Patríque compar Unice,
   Cum Spiritu Paráclito,
   Regnans per omne sáeculum.

AFTER THE HYMN.

℣. Di - ri - ga - tur Do - mi-ne o - ra - ti - o me-a, a, a...........
℞. Si - cut in - cen-sum in conspectu tu - - o, o, o...........

MAGNIFICAT.

1. Magni - - - - *fl - cat,* ánima....... *me - a Dó - mi-num.*

2. Et ex - - - ultávit spíritus *me - us,* in Deo salu - *tá - ri me - o.*

3. Quia respéxit humilitátem, ancíllæ *su-æ:* ecce énim ex hoc beátam me dicent,
   [omnes gene-*rá-ti-o-nes.*
4. Quia fecit mihi magna, qui *pótens est:* et sanctum *no-men e-jus.*
5. Et misericórdia ejus a progénie, in pro-*gén-ies,* timén-*ti-bus e-um.*
6. Fecit poténtiam, in bráchio *su-o,* dispérsit supérbos, mente *cór-dis su-i.*
7. Depósuit poténtes de *se-de;* et exal-*tá-vit hú-mi-les.*
8. Esúriéntes implévit *bo-nis;* et dívites di-*mí-sit iná-nes.*
9. Suscépit Israel púerum *su-um;* recordátus miseri-*cór-diæ su-æ.*
10. Sicut locútus est, ad Patres *no-stros;* Abraham, et sémini *ejus in sæ-cu-la.*
11. Gloria Patri, et *Fi-lio;* et Spiri-*tu-i San-cto.*
12. Sicut erat in princípio, et nunc et *sem-per;* et in sæcula sæcu-*lo-rum. A-men.*

AFTER THE "MAGNIFICAT."

V. Dóminus vo - - - - bís - cum. (**AFTER THE COLLECT**) V. Be - - - ne - di - cá - mus
R. Et cum spíritu . . . . tu - o. R. A - men. R. De - - - - - - - o

Dó - - - - - mi - no.
o - - - gra - - ti - as.

THEN THE CELEBRANT SINGS:

V. Fidélium ánimæ per mi -

sericórdiam Dei requiéscant in . . . . pa - ce. R. A - - men.

V. Dóminus det nobis suam pa - cem. R. Et vitam ætérnam. A - men.

Then follows immediately one of the Anthems of the B. V. M., according to season. From Advent till Candlemas excl., "*Alma;*" till Holy Thursday, "*Ave,*" from Easter to Trinity Sunday, "*Regina Coeli;*" from Trinity till Advent, "*Salve.*"

The Four Antiphons B. V. M.

I. ALMA REDEMPTORIS MATER.

1. Al - ma, al - ma, al - - - - - ma, Re-dempto - ris
2. Sur-ge-re qui cu - rat po - - - - pu - lo, tu quæ ge - nu -
3. Vir - go pri - us, ac.........po-ste -ri - us, Ga-bri -é - lis

ma - ter, Quæ per-vi - a cœ - li, Por - ta ma-nes et Stel - la
is - ti, Na - tu - ra mi -ran - te, Tu - um san - ctum Ge - ni -
ab ó- re, Su - mens il - lud A - ve Pec - ca - to - rum mi - se -

ma - ris, Suc-cu - re ca - den - ti. Por - ta ma - nes et
to - rem, Tu - um san - ctum ge - ni-torem. Tu - um san - ctum
re - re, Pec - ca - to - rum mi - se - rere. Pec - ca - to - rum

Stel - la ma - ris, Suc - cur - re ca - den - ti.
ge - ni - to - rem, Tu - um san - ctum ge - ni - torem.
mi - se - re - re, Pec - ca - to - rum mi - se - rere.

IN ADVENT. ℣. Angelus Dómini nuntiávit Mariæ. ℞. Et concépit de Spíritu Sancto.
AFTER ADVENT. ℣. Post partum Virgo invioláta pérmansisti. ℞. Dei génitrix in-
tercede pro nobis. ℣. Oremus, etc. ℞. Amen.   35

II. AVE REGINA.

A - ve, A - ve Re - gi - na, Re - gi - na cœ - lo - rum.   A - ve

Do - mi-na,   A - - - ve Do - mi - na, Do - mi - na An - ge - lo - rum.

Sal - ve ra - dix, Sal - ve por - ta, Ex qua mundo lux est or - ta.

Gau - de Vir - go glo - ri - o - sa, Su - per om - nes spe - ci - o - sa, Va -

AVE REGINA. Concluded.

le, O val - de de - co - ra, Et pro no - bis Chris-tum ex - o - ra,

Va - le O val - de de - co - ra, Et pro no - bis Christum ex - o - ra.

℣. Dignáre me laudáre te, Virgo sacráta.　℞. Da míhi virtútem contra hostes tuos.
After the prayer: Amen.

III. REGINA CŒLI.

Re - gi - na cœ - li, Re - gi - na cœ - li, læ - ta - re, læ - ta - re, Al -

le - lu - ja. Qui-a quem me-ru-is-ti, meru - is - ti por - ta - re, Al - le - lu -

REGINA CŒLI. Concluded.

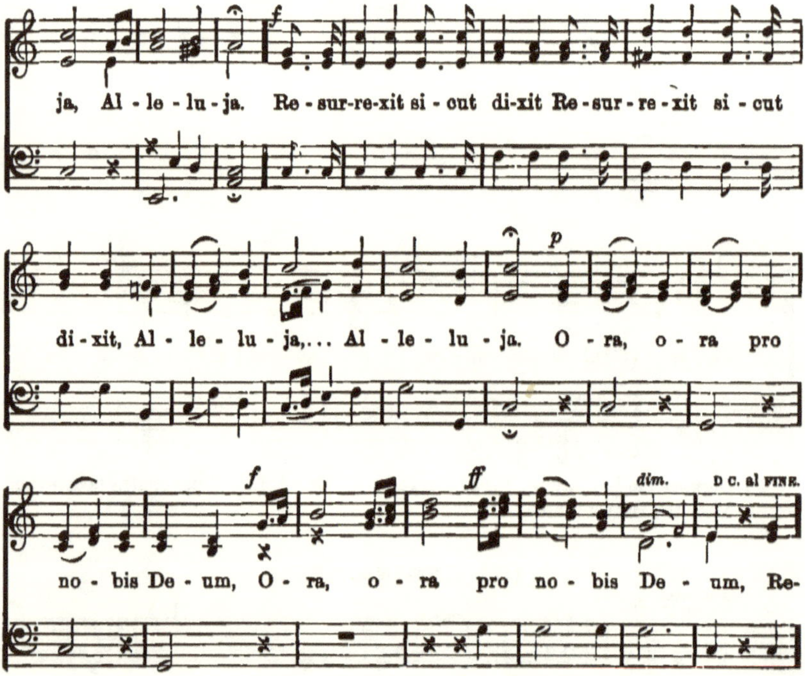
f
ja, Al - le - lu - ja. Re - sur-re-xit si - cut di-xit Re - sur - re - xit si - cut
p
di - xit, Al - le - lu - ja,... Al - le - lu - ja. O - ra, o - ra pro
f
ff
dim.
D C. al FINE.
no - bis De - um, O - ra, o - ra pro no - bis De - um, Re-

℣. Gaude, et lætáre, Virgo Maria. Allelúja. ℟. Quia surréxit Dóminus vére, al- [lelúja.
After the prayer: Amen.

IV. SALVE REGINA.

mf Moderato.
1. { Sal - ve Re - gi - na, Ma - ter Mi - se - ri - cor - diæ. 2. Ad te cla-
Vi - ta, dul - ce - do, Et spes no - stra, sal - ve. 3. Ei - a...

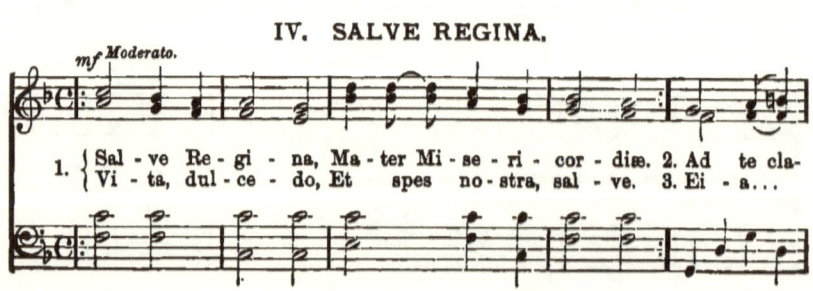

SALVE REGINA. Coñcluded.

ma - mus, ex - u - les fi - lii E - væ, ad te su - spi -
er - go ad - vo - ca - ta no - stra, il - los tu - os

ra - mus, ge - men - tes et flou - - tes, in hac la-cry-
mi - se - ri - cor - des o - cu - los ad nos - -

ma - rum va - lle. } 4. Et Je - sum be - ne - dic - tum fru-ctum ven - tris
con - ver - te. } no - bis post hoc ex - i - li - um os-

tu - i. } 5. O cle-mens! O pi - a! O dul - cis Vir - go Ma - ri - a!
ten - de. }

℣. Ora pro nobis, sancta Dei Génitrix.   ℞. Ut dígni efficiámur promissiónibus
After the Prayer: Amen.   [Christi.

AFTER THE ANTIPHON AND PRAYER:

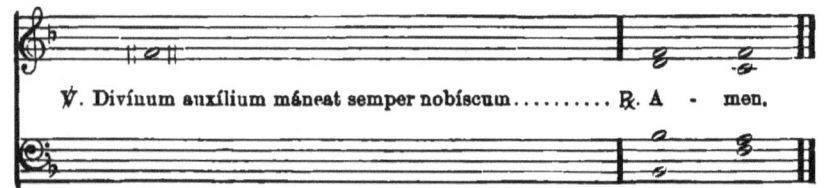

℣. Divínum auxílium máneat semper nobíscum .... ℞. A - men.

Benediction.

O SALUTARIS HOSTIA.

Andante. dolce.

1. O   sa - lu - tá - ris   Hós - - tia, Quæ cœ - li   pan - dis
2. U - ni tri - nó - que Dó - - mino, Sit   sem - pi - tér - na

ós - - ti - um; Bel - la   pre - munt ho - sti - - li - a,
glo - ri - a   Qui vi - tam si - ne   ter - - mi - no,

Da   ró - bur   fer   au - xi - - li - um.
No - bis do - net   in   pa - - tri - a.   A - - men.

TANTUM ERGO, No. 1.

Tan - tum er - go Sa - cra - mén - tum, Ve - ne - ré - mur cér -
Ge - ni - tó - ri, Ge - ni - tó - que, Laus.... et ju - bi - lá -

nu - i..........; Et an - ti - quum do - cu - mén - tum, No - vo
ti - o..........; Sa - lus hon - or vir - tus quo - que, Sit et

ce - dat ri - tu - i..........; Præ-stet fi - des sup - ple - mén - tum,
be - ne - dic - ti - o........; Pro - ce - den - ti ab u - tro - que.

Sén - su - um de - féc - tu - i.
Com - par sit lau - da - ti - o. A - - - men.

℣. Panem de Cœlo, etc., see page 42.

TANTUM ERGO, No. 2.

5. Tan-tum er - go Sa-cra-mentum, Ve - ne - re - mur cer - nu - i;
6. Ge - ni - to - ri, Ge - ni - to - que, Laus et ju - bi - la - ti - o,

Et an - ti - quum do - cu - mentum, No - vo ce - dat ri - tu - i;
Sa - lus ho - nor vir - tus quo - que, Sit et be - ne - dic - ti - o.

Præs-tet fi - des sup-ple - mentum, Sensu - um de - fec - tu - i.
Pro - ce - den - ti ab u - tro-que. Compar sit lau - da - ti - o.   A - men.

1. Pange lingua, gloriósi
Córporis mystérium,
Sanguinisque pretiósi,
Quem in mundi prétium
Fructus ventris generósi
Rex effúdit géntium.

2. Nobis datus, nobis natus
Ex intácta Virgine,

Et in mundo conversátus,
Sparso verbi sémine,
Sui moras incolátus
Miro clausit órdine.

3. In suprémæ nocte cœnæ
Recúmbens cum frátribus,
Observáta lege plene
Cibis in legálibus,

Cibum turbæ duodénæ
Se dat suis mánibus.

4. Verbum caro, panem verum
Verbo carnem éfficit:
Fitque sanguis Christi merum:
Et si sensus déficit,
Ad firmándum cor sincérum
Sola fides súfficit.

In Easter time add: "Alleluja."

℣. Panem de cóelo præstitísti .... e - is. (AFTER THE PRAYER:)
℞. Omnem delectaméntum in se ha - - - ben-tem. ℞. A - - men.

After Benediction the "Laudate Dominum" (see page 30) may be repeated.

" Hymns. *

1. THE STAR OF THE SEA.

p Andante con moto.

1. O pur - est of creatures, sweet Moth - er, sweet Maid! The one spot-less
2. Deep night hath come down on this rough-spo-ken world, And the ban-ners of
3. Oh! bliss - ful and calm was the won - der - ful rest That thou gav - est thy
4. Oh! shine on us bright-er than ev - er, then, shine! For the primest of

mf

womb where-in Je - sus was laid, Dark night has come down on us,
dark-ness are bold - ly un-furled; And the tem - pest-tossed Church, all her
God in thy vir - gin - al breast; For the heav - en He left He found
hon - ors, dear Moth - er! is thine; "Con-ceived with-out sin," thy new

Moth - er, and we Look out for thy shin-ing, sweet Star of the Sea.
eyes are on thee: They look to thy shin-ing, sweet Star of the Sea.
heav - en in thee, And He shone in thy shin-ing, sweet Star of the Sea.
ti - tle shall be, Clear light from thy birth spring, sweet Star of the Sea.

* For the words of these hymns see "The New Sunday School Companion," page 211-244.

2. TOTA PULCHRA.

To - ta pul - chra es Ma - ri - a, to - ta pul - chra, to - ta

pul - chra, es Ma - ri - a, et ma - cu - la o - ri - gi - na - lis, et

ma - cu - la o - ri - gi - na - lis non est in te. Tu glo - ri - a Je -

ru - sa - lem, tu lœ - ti - ti - a Is - ra - el, Tu ho - no - ri - fi -

cen - ti - a po - pu - li nos - tri, tu ad - vo - ca - ta pec - ca -

TOTA PULCHRA. Continued.

to - rum, tu ad - vo - ca - - - - - - ta,

tu ad - vo - ca - ta, tu ad - vo - ca - ta pec - ca - to - - rum.

O Ma - ri - a, O Ma - ri - a, Vir - go pru - den -

- tis - si - ma, Ma - - ter cle - men - tis - si - ma,

O - ra pro no - bis, O - ra pro no - bis,

O - ra pro no - bis, O - ra pro no - bis. In - ter -

TOTA PULCHRA. Concluded.

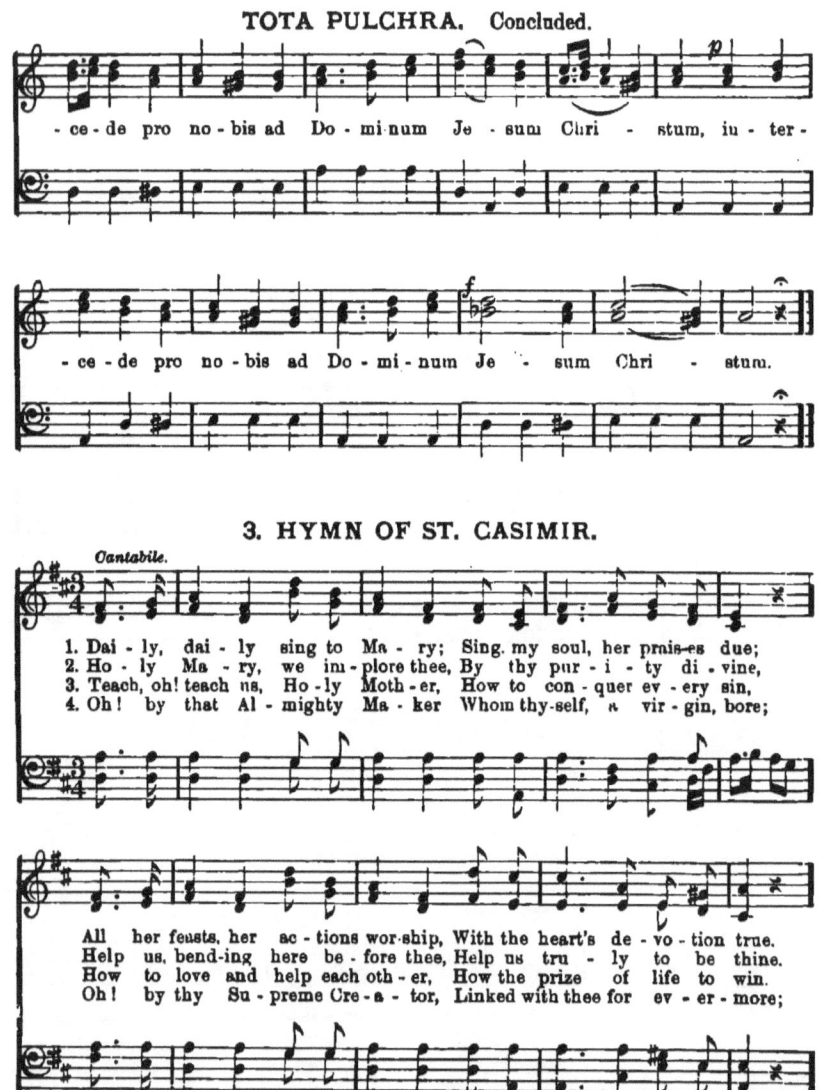

-ce - de pro no - bis ad Do - mi-num Je - sum Chri - stum, iu - ter-

-ce - de pro no - bis ad Do - mi - num Je - sum Chri - stum.

3. HYMN OF ST. CASIMIR.

Cantabile.

1. Dai - ly, dai - ly sing to Ma - ry; Sing, my soul, her prais-es due;
2. Ho - ly Ma - ry, we im - plore thee, By thy pur - i - ty di - vine,
3. Teach, oh! teach us, Ho - ly Moth - er, How to con - quer ev - ery sin,
4. Oh! by that Al - mighty Ma - ker Whom thy-self, a vir - gin, bore;

All her feasts, her ac - tions wor-ship, With the heart's de - vo - tion true.
Help us, bend-ing here be - fore thee, Help us tru - ly to be thine.
How to love and help each oth - er, How the prize of life to win.
Oh! by thy Su - preme Cre-a - tor, Linked with thee for ev - er - more;

HYMN OF ST. CASIMIR. Concluded.

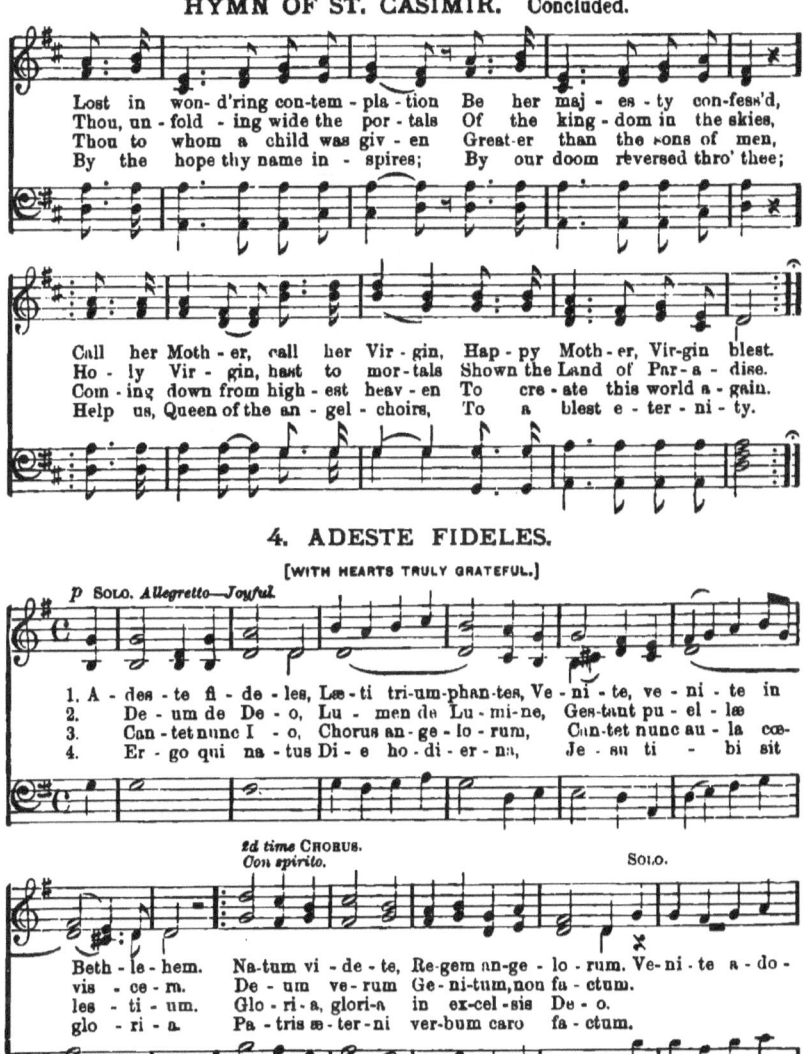

Lost in won- d'ring con-tem - pla - tion   Be her maj - es - ty con-fess'd,
Thou, un -fold - ing wide the por - tals Of the king - dom in the skies,
Thou to whom a child was giv - en   Great-er than the sons of men,
By the hope thy name in - spires;   By our doom reversed thro' thee;

Call her Moth - er, call her Vir - gin, Hap - py Moth - er, Vir-gin blest.
Ho - ly Vir - gin, hast to mor-tals Shown the Land of Par - a - dise.
Com - ing down from high - est heav - en To cre - ate this world a - gain.
Help us, Queen of the an - gel - choirs, To a blest e - ter - ni - ty.

4. ADESTE FIDELES.

[WITH HEARTS TRULY GRATEFUL.]

p SOLO. *Allegretto—Joyful.*

1. A - des - te fi - de - les, Læ - ti tri-um-phan-tes, Ve - ni - te, ve - ni - te in
2.   De - um de De - o, Lu - men de Lu - mi-ne, Ges-tant pu - el - læ
3.   Can -tet nunc I - o, Chorus an - ge - lo - rum, Can-tet nunc au - la cœ-
4.   Er - go qui na - tus Di - e ho - di - er - na, Je - su ti - bi sit

2d time CHORUS.
Con spirito.   SOLO.

Beth - le - hem. Na-tum vi - de - te, Re-gem an-ge - lo - rum. Ve-ni - te a - do -
vis - ce - m. De - um ve - rum Ge - ni-tum,non fa - ctum.
les - ti - um. Glo - ri - a, glori-a in ex-cel - sis De - o.
glo - ri - a. Pa - tris æ - ter -ni ver-bum caro fa - ctum.

ADESTE FIDELES. Concluded.

- re - mus, Ve-ni-te a - do - re-mus; Ve-ni-te a-do-re-mus Do-mi-num.

To this air the following English words also can be sung:

1. With hearts truly grateful
   Come, all ye faithful,
To Jesus, to Jesus in Bethlehem:
   See Christ your Saviour,
   Heaven's greatest favor.

Cho.—Let's hasten to adore Him,
   Let's hasten to adore Him,
   Let's hasten to adore Him, our God and
      King.

2. God to God equal,
   Light of light eternal;
Carried in Virgin's ever spotless womb;

He all preceded,
Begotten, not created.—Cho.

3. Angels now praise Him,
   Loud their voices raising,
The heavenly mansions with joy now ring,
   To Him Who's most holy,
   Be honor, praise and glory.—Cho.

4. To Jesus, this day born,
   Grateful homage return;
'Tis He, Who all heavenly gifts does bring;
   Word increated,
   To our flesh united.—Cho.

5. THE VIRGIN MOTHER.

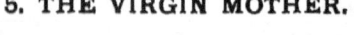

mf A llegretto.

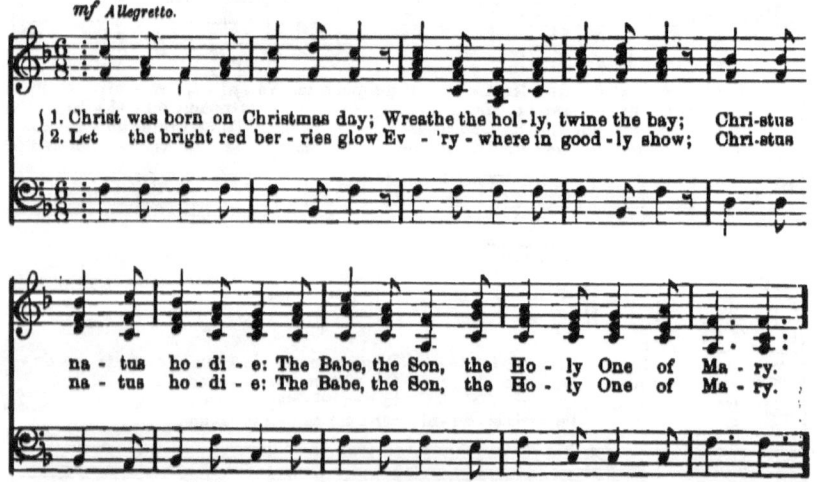

{ 1. Christ was born on Christmas day; Wreathe the hol-ly, twine the bay;   Chri-stus
{ 2. Let   the bright red ber-ries glow Ev - 'ry-where in good-ly show;   Chri-stus

na - tus ho-di-e: The Babe, the Son, the Ho-ly One of Ma-ry.
na - tus ho-di-e: The Babe, the Son, the Ho-ly One of Ma-ry.

THE VIRGIN MOTHER. Continued.

He is born to set us free,
Christian men, re - joice and sing; 'Tis the birth - day of a King,

Ex Ma - ri - a, Vir - gi - ne; The God, the Lord by all a -
Ex Ma - ri - a, Vir - gi - ne; The God, the Lord by all a -

dored for - ev - er. 3. Night of sad - ness, Morn of glad-ness, Ev - er -
dored for - ev - er.

more; Ev - er, ev - er: Af - ter ma - ny trou - bles sore;

Morn of glad-ness, ev - er-more and ev - er-more; Mid-night scarce-ly

THE VIRGIN MOTHER. Concluded.

passed and o - ver, Draw-ing to this ho - ly morn, Ver - y ear - ly,

ver - y ear - ly Christ was born. 4. Sing out with bliss, His name is

piu lento. *a tempo.*

this, E - man - u - el: As was fore - told, In days of old, By

Ga - bri - el. Mid-night scarce-ly passed and o - ver, Draw-ing to this

rall.

ho - ly morn, Ver - y ear - ly, ver - y ear - ly Christ was born.

6. WITH WONDERING AWE.

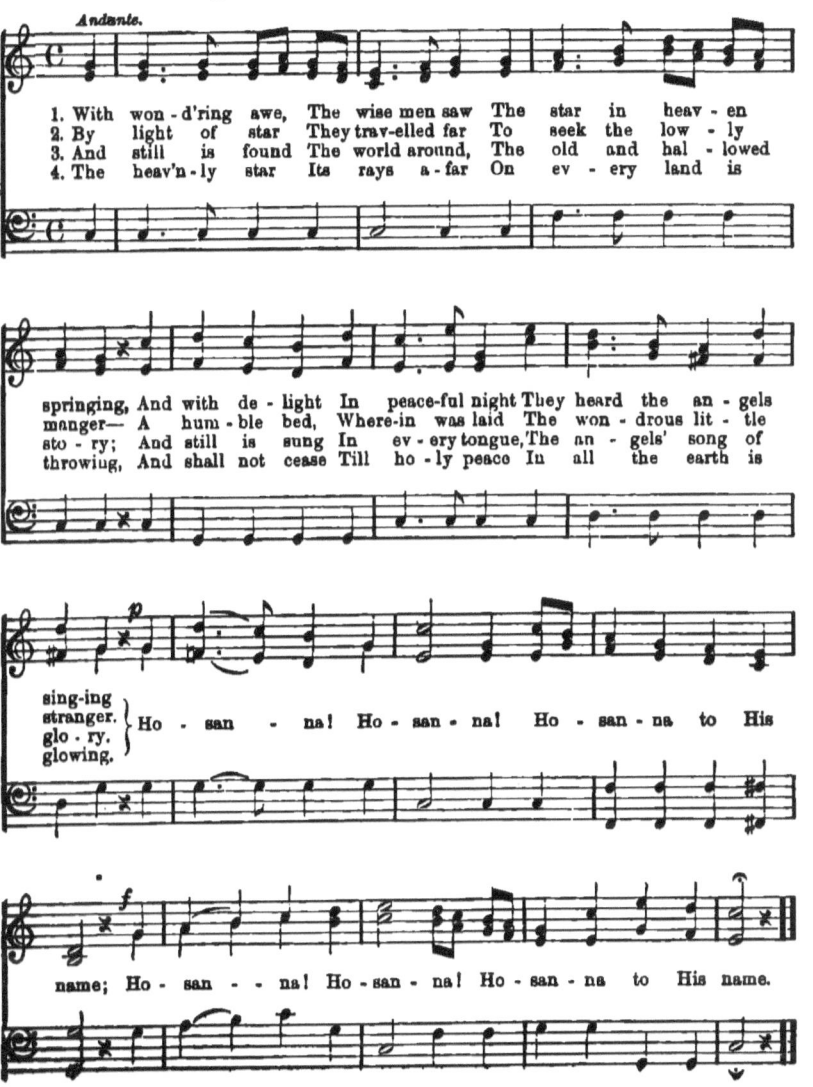

Andante.

1. With won - d'ring awe, The wise men saw The star in heav - en
2. By light of star They trav-elled far To seek the low - ly
3. And still is found The world around, The old and hal - lowed
4. The heav'n - ly star Its rays a - far On ev - ery land is

springing, And with de - light In peace-ful night They heard the an - gels
manger— A hum - ble bed, Where-in was laid The won - drous lit - tle
sto - ry; And still is sung In ev - ery tongue, The an - gels' song of
throwing, And shall not cease Till ho - ly peace In all the earth is

sing-ing. } Ho - san - na! Ho - san - na! Ho - san - na to His
stranger. }
glo - ry. }
glowing. }

name; Ho - san - - na! Ho - san - na! Ho - san - na to His name.

7. STABAT MATER.

Adagio molto.

1. { Sta - bat ma - ter do - lo - ro - sa, Jux - ta cru - cem
   { Cu - jus a - ni - mam ge - men - tem Con - tri - sta - tam
2. { O quam tri - stis et af - fli - cta Fu - it il - la
   { Quæ mœ - re - bat et do - le - bat, Pi - a Ma - ter,

1. { la - cry - mo - sa, Dum pen - de - bat Fi - li - us.
   { et do - len - tem Per - tran - si - vit gla - di - us.
2. { be - ne - di - cta Ma - ter U - ni - ge - ni - ti.
   { dum vi - de - bat Na - ti pœ - nas in - cly - ti.

3. Quis est homo qui non fleret,
   Matrem Christi si videret
   In tanto supplicio !
   Quis non posset contristari,
   Christi Matrem contemplari
   Dolentem cum Filio ?

4. Pro peccatis suæ gentis
   Vidit Jesum in tormentis,
   Et flagellis subditum,
   Vidit suum dulcem Natum
   Morieudo desolatam,
   Dum emisit spiritum.

5. Eia, Mater, fons amoris,
   Me sentire vim doloris
   Fac, ut tecum lugeam.

Fac, ut ardeat cor meum
In amando Christum Deum,
Ut sibi complaceam.

6. Sancta Mater, istud agas,
   Crucifixi fige plagas
   Cordi meo valide.
   Tui Nati vulnerati,
   Tam dignati pro me pati,
   Pœnas mecum divide.

7. Fac me tecum pie flere,
   Crucifixo condolere,
   Donec ego vixero.
   Juxta Crucem tecum stare,
   Et me tibi sociare
   In planctu æsidero.

To this air the following English words may also be sung :

1. At the Cross her station keeping,
   Stood the mournful Mother weeping,
   Close to Jesus to the last:
   Through her heart His sorrow sharing,
   All His bitter anguish bearing
   Now at length the sword had passed.

2. Oh, how sad and sore distressed
   Was that Mother highly blest
   Of the sole-begotten One!
   Christ above in torment hangs;
   She beneath beholds the pangs
   Of her dying glorious Son.

3. Is there one who would not weep,
   Whelmed in miseries so deep
   Christ's dear Mother to behold !
   Can the human heart refrain
   From partaking in her pain,
   In that mother's pain untold !

4. Bruised, derided, cursed, defiled,
   She beheld her tender Child
   All with bloody scourges rent;

For the sins of His own nation,
Saw Him hang in desolation,
Till his spirit forth He sent.

5. O thou Mother! fount of love!
   Touch my spirit from above,
   Make my heart with thine accord:
   Make me feel as thou hast felt:
   Make my soul to glow and melt
   With the love of Christ my Lord.

6. Holy mother! pierce me through;
   In my heart each wound renew
   Of my Saviour crucified;
   Let me share with thee his pain,
   Who for all my sins was slain,
   Who for me in torments died.

7. Let me mingle tears with thee,
   Mourning Him Who mourned for me,
   All the days that I may live:
   By the Cross with thee to stay,
   There with thee to weep and pray,
   Is all I ask of thee to give.

8. SOUL OF JESUS.

Andantino.

1. Soul of Je - sus, make me ho - ly, Make me con-trite. meek and low - ly;
2. Save me, Bod - y of my Lord, Save a sin - ner vile ab - horred;

Soul most stain-less, Soul di - vine, Cleanse this sordid soul of mine; Hal - low
Sa - cred Bod - y, wan and worn, Bruised and mangled, crush'd and torn; Pierc-ed

this pol - lu - ted soul, Pur - ri - fy it, make it whole; Soul of Je - sus,
hands and feet and side, Scourg'd, in - sult - ed, cru - ci-fied: Save me, to the

hal - low me; Mi - se - re - re Do - mi - ne! 3. Mi - se - re - re!
cross I flee; Mi - se - re - re Do - mi - ne!

let me be, nev - er part - ed, Lord from Thee; Guard me from my

SOUL OF JESUS. Concluded.

ruth - less foe, Save me from e - ter - nal woe. In the dread - ful

judg - ment day, Be thy cross my hope and stay; When the hour of

death is near, And my spir - it faints for fear, Call me with Thy

voice of love, Place me near to Thee a - bove, With thine

an - gel hosts to raise Nev - er end - ing hymns of praise.

9. O FILII ET FILIÆ.

Con moto.

1-5. Al - le - lu - ia! Al - le - lu - - ia! Al - le - lu -

ia! ......
1. Ye sons and daugh-ters of the Lord, The
2. All in the ear - ly morn - ing gray, Went
3. Of spi - ces pure a pre - cious store In
4. Then straightway one in white they see, Who
5. Now let us praise the Lord most high, And

King of Heav'n, the King a - dored, From death this
ho - ly wom - en on their way, To see the
their pure hands these wom - en bore, To a - noint the
saith, "Ye seek the Lord; but He Is risen, and
strive His name to mag - ni - fy On this great

day Him - self re - stored. Al - le - lu - - - - ia! ......
tomb where Je - sus lay. Al - le - lu - - - - ia! ......
sa - cred Bod - y o'er. Al - le - lu - - - - ia! ......
gone to Gal - i - lee." Al - le - lu - - - - ia! ......
day, through earth and sky. Al - le - lu - - - - ia! ......

10. INVOCATIO S. SPIRITUS.

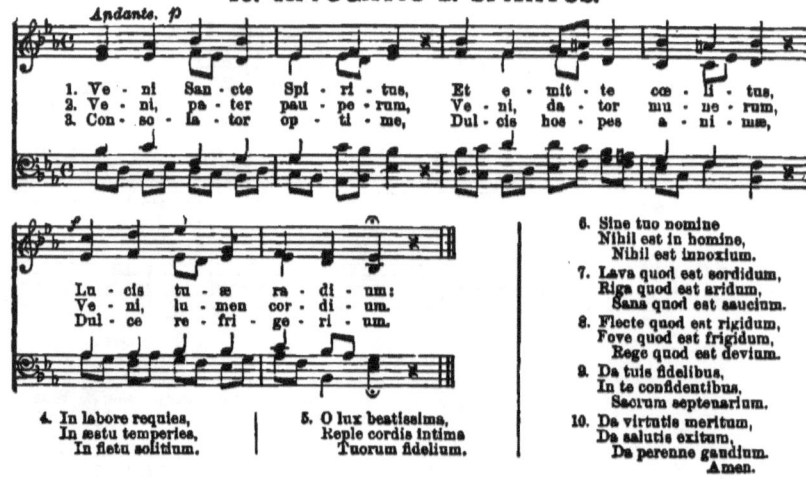

1. Ve - ni San - cte Spi - ri - tus, Et e - mit - te cœ - li - tus,
2. Ve - ni, pa - ter pau - pe - rum, Ve - ni, da - tor mu - ne - rum,
3. Con - so - la - tor op - ti - me, Dul - cis hos - pes a - ni - mæ,

Lu - cis tu - æ ra - di - um:
Ve - ni, lu - men cor - di - um.
Dul - ce re - fri - ge - ri - um.

6. Sine tuo nomine
Nihil est in homine,
Nihil est innoxium.

7. Lava quod est sordidum,
Riga quod est aridum,
Sana quod est saucium.

8. Flecte quod est rigidum,
Fove quod est frigidum,
Rege quod est devium.

9. Da tuis fidelibus,
In te confidentibus,
Sacrum septenarium.

10. Da virtutis meritum,
Da salutis exitum,
Da perenne gaudium.
Amen.

4. In labore requies,
In æstu temperies,
In fletu solitium.

5. O lux beatissima,
Reple cordis intima
Tuorum fidelium.

11. COME, HOLY GHOST.

1. Come, Ho - ly Ghost, Cre - a - tor blest, And in our hearts take
2. O Com - fort - er,.... to Thee we cry; Thou heav'n-ly Gift of
3. Drive far a - way.. our dead - ly foe, And peace for ev - er -
4. Praise we the Fa - - ther and the Son, And Ho - ly Spir - it,

up Thy rest; Come with Thy grace.. and heav'n-ly aid, To fill the
God most high; Thou fount of life.... and fire of love, And sweet a -
more be - stow: If Thou be our.... pre - vent - ing guide, No e - vil
Three in One; And may the Son.... on us be - stow The gifts that

hearts which Thou hast made, To fill the hearts which Thou hast made.
noint - ing from a - bove, And sweet a - noint - ing from a - bove.
can our steps be - tide, No e - vil can our steps be - tide.
from the Spir - it flow, The gifts that from the Spir - it flow.

12. SEE THE PARACLETE DESCENDING.

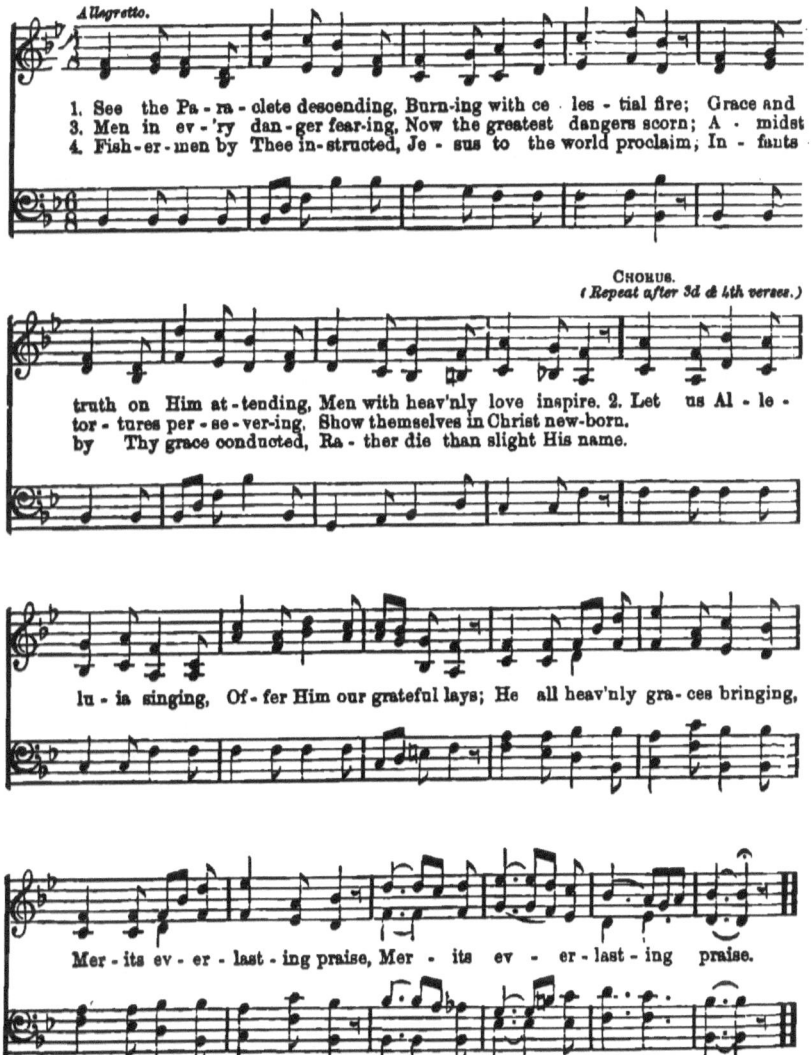

Allegretto.

1. See the Pa - ra - clete descending, Burn-ing with ce · les - tial fire; Grace and
3. Men in ev - 'ry dan - ger fear-ing, Now the greatest dangers scorn; A · midst
4. Fish - er - men by Thee in-structed, Je - sus to the world proclaim; In - fants

CHORUS.
(Repeat after 3d & 4th verses.)

truth on Him at - tending, Men with heav'nly love inspire. 2. Let us Al - le -
tor - tures per - se - ver-ing. Show themselves in Christ new-born.
by Thy grace conducted, Ra - ther die than slight His name.

lu - ia singing, Of - fer Him our grateful lays; He all heav'nly gra - ces bringing,

Mer - its ev - er - last - ing praise, Mer - its ev - er - last - ing praise.

13. AVE, MARIS STELLA.

Andante. p

1. A - ve, ma - ris stel - la, De - i ma - ter al - ma,
2. Su - mens il - lud A - ve, Ga - bri - e - lis o - re,
3. Sol - ve vin - cla re - is, Pro - fer lu - men cæ - cis,
4. Mon - stra te esse ma - trem, Su - mat per te pre - ces,

At - que sem - per vir - go, Fe - lix cœ - li por - ta.
Fun - da nos in pa - ce, Mu - tans E - væ no - men.
Ma - la no - stra pel - le, Bo - na cun - cta po - sce.
Qui pro no - bis na - tus Tu - lit es - se tu - us.

5. Virgo singularis,
Inter omnes mitis,
Nos culpis solutos
Mites fac et castos.

6. Vitam præsta puram,
Iter para tutum,
Ut videntes Jesum,
Semper collætemur.

7. Sit laus Deo Patri,
Summo Christo decus,
Spiritui Sancto,
Tribus honor unus. Amen.

14. BRIGHT MOTHER OF OUR MAKER.

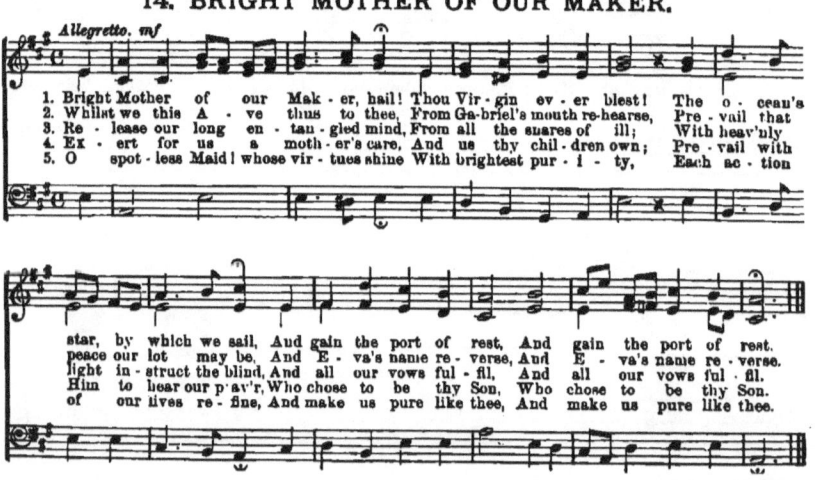

Allegretto. mf

1. Bright Mother of our Mak - er, hail! Thou Vir - gin ev - er blest! The o - cean's
2. Whilst we this A - ve thus to thee, From Ga-briel's mouth re-hearse, Pre - vail that
3. Re - lease our long en - tan - gled mind, From all the snares of ill; With heav'nly
4. Ex - ert for us a moth - er's care, And us thy chil - dren own; Pre - vail with
5. O spot - less Maid! whose vir - tues shine With brightest pur - i - ty, Each ac - tion

star, by which we sail, And gain the port of rest, And gain the port of rest.
peace our lot may be, And E - va's name re - verse, And E - va's name re - verse.
light in - struct the blind, And all our vows ful - fil, And all our vows ful - fil.
Him to hear our p'av'r, Who chose to be thy Son, Who chose to be thy Son.
of our lives re - fine, And make us pure like thee, And make us pure like thee.

15. DEAREST MOTHER.

Andantino. *p*

1. We come, dearest Mother, with fondest de - vo-tion, To place on thy shrine no
2. Hail, high - est and holiest bright lil - y of heaven, In the garden of God thou
3. The rose and the lil - y of earth's early spring-time, Mary, dear Mother, we

pearls of the sea: The pearls of our hearts,—the tru - est af - fec - tions,
reign-est su - preme; Chos'n ves - sel of honor, Im - ma - cu - late ev - er,
wreathe for thee now, Draw near - er, bright angels, with songs of glad - ness,

Dear - est and best, we bring un - to thee, Dear-est and best, we
Moth - er of Je - sus! we hail thee our Queen, Moth-er of Je - sus! we
As we place flow'rs on our dear Mother's brow, As we place flow'rs on our

p   *pp*

bring un - to thee.
hail thee our Queen. } O Ma - ry, hear our prayer, O Ma - ry, hear our prayer.
dear Mother's brow.

16. ORA PRO ME.

1. A - ve Ma - ri - a! bright and pure,   Hear, oh, hear me
2. A - ve Ma - ri - a! Queen of Heav'n,   Teach, oh, teach me
3. Then shall I, if thou, O Ma - ry,   Art my strong sup-
4. When my eyes are slow - ly clos - ing,   And I fade from

when I pray,   Pains and pleas-ures try the pil - grim On him
to o - bey,   Lead me on thro' fierce temp-ta - tions Stand and
port and stay,   Fear nor feel the three - fold dan - ger, Stand-ing
earth a - way,   And when death, the stern de - stroy - er, Claims my

long and drear-y way.   Fears and per - ils are a - round me,
meet me in the way.   When I fail and faint, my Moth - er,
forth in dread ar - ray.   Now and ev - er shield and guard me,
bod - y as his prey,   Claim my soul, and then, sweet Ma - ry,
A - ve Ma-

ri - a! bright and pure,   O - ra pro me,   o - ra pro me.

17. MAGNIFICAT.

Chorus.—*Maestoso.*

Glo - ry to God! Angels hosts are sing - ing, Is - rael's Ho - ly One,

FINE.

has for us be - come Ma - ry's Son,—Peace on earth to us bring - ing.

Solo.—*Con moto.*

1. O mag-ni - fy the Lord! Break forth in songs, my voice. In my
2. My low - li - ness He sought, On me His eyes He cast. And in
3. The might-y ones He spurns, The humble He re - ceives, Fills the

Sav - iour a - dored, My spir - it doth re - joice, While
me He has wrought A won - der un - sur - passed! His
soul that yearns; The rich in want He leaves. To

MAGNIFICAT. Concluded.

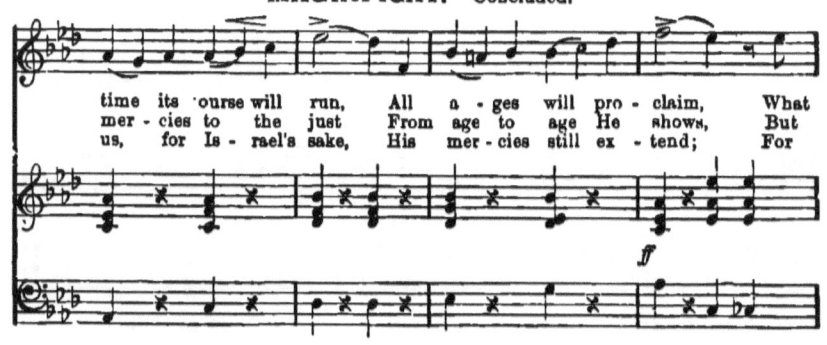

time its course will run, All a - ges will pro - claim, What
mer - cies to the just From age to age He shows, But
us, for Is - rael's sake, His mer - cies still ex - tend; For

After each verse repeat "Glory to God."

God hath in me done, And bless - ed call.... my name.
hum - bles in the dust His proud and haught - y foes.
A - bram, as He spake, His love shall nev - er end.

18. AVE SANCTISSIMA.

Moderato.

1. A - ve Sanc-tis - si - ma, We lift our souls to thee, O - ra pro
3. A - ve Pur - is - si - ma, List to thy children's pray'r, Au - di Ma -

AVE SANCTISSIMA. Concluded.

1. no - bis! 'Tis night-fall on the sea.   Watch us while shad-ows lie,
3. ri - a! And take us to thy care.   When darkness comes o'er us,

1. Far o'er the wa - ter spread, Hear the heart's lone -ly sigh, Thine too hath bled.
3. Whilst here on earth we stay, Thy light shine be - fore us, Guide of our way.

(2d verse repeats after the 3d.)

2. Thou that hast look'd on death, Aid us when death is near; Whis - per of

2. heav'n to faith, Sweet mother, Sweet mother hear, O - ra pro no - bis, The

2. wave must rock our sleep, O - ra ma - ter, O - ra, star of the deep.

19. O SANCTISSIMA.

Adagio.

1. O sanc - tis - si - ma,   O   pu - ris - si - ma,   Dul - cis
2. To - ta   pul - chra   es,   O   Ma - ri - - a,   Et   ma -
3. Si - cut li - li - um,   in - ter spi - - nas,   Sic   Ma -

Vir - go Ma - ri - - a.   Ma - ter a - ma - ta,
cu - la non est in te.   Ma - ter a - ma - ta,
ria in - ter fi - lias.   Ma - ter a - ma - ta,

in - te - me - ra - ta,   O - ra,   o - ra pro no - bis.
in - te - me - ra - ta,   O - ra,   o - ra pro no - bis.
in - te - me - ra - ta,   O - ra,   o - ra pro no - bis.

20. HAIL, HEAVENLY QUEEN.

Cantabile.

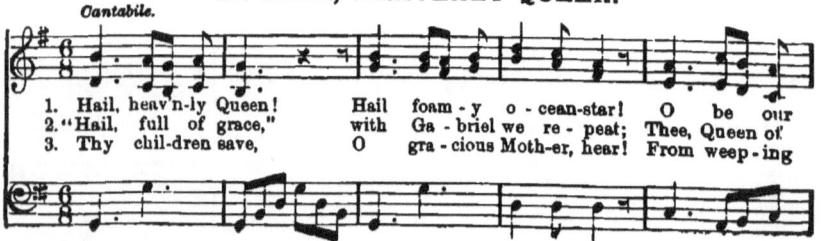

1. Hail, heav'n-ly Queen!   Hail foam - y o - cean-star!   O   be   our
2. "Hail, full of grace,"   with Ga - briel we re - peat;   Thee, Queen of
3. Thy chil-dren save,   O   gra - cious Moth-er, hear!   From weep - ing

HAIL, HEAVENLY QUEEN. Concluded.

guide, dif - fuse thy beams a - far;.... Oh, Moth-er of God! a -
heav'n, from him we learn to greet; Then give.... us peace, which
eyes, oh, deign to wipe the tear! Our hum - ble pray'rs to

bove all vir-gins blest, Hail, hap - py gate of heav'n's e-ter - nal rest.
heav'n a-lone can give, And dead thro' Eve, thro' Ma - ry let us live.
God thy Son pre - sent, Whose life and blood for sin - ful man were spent.

CHORUS.

Hail, foam - y o - cean-star! Sweet heav'n - ly Queen!

1st time. *2nd time.*

O be our guide to end - less joys se - rene.
O be our guide to end - less joys se - - rene.

21. ON THIS DAY, O BEAUTIFUL MOTHER.

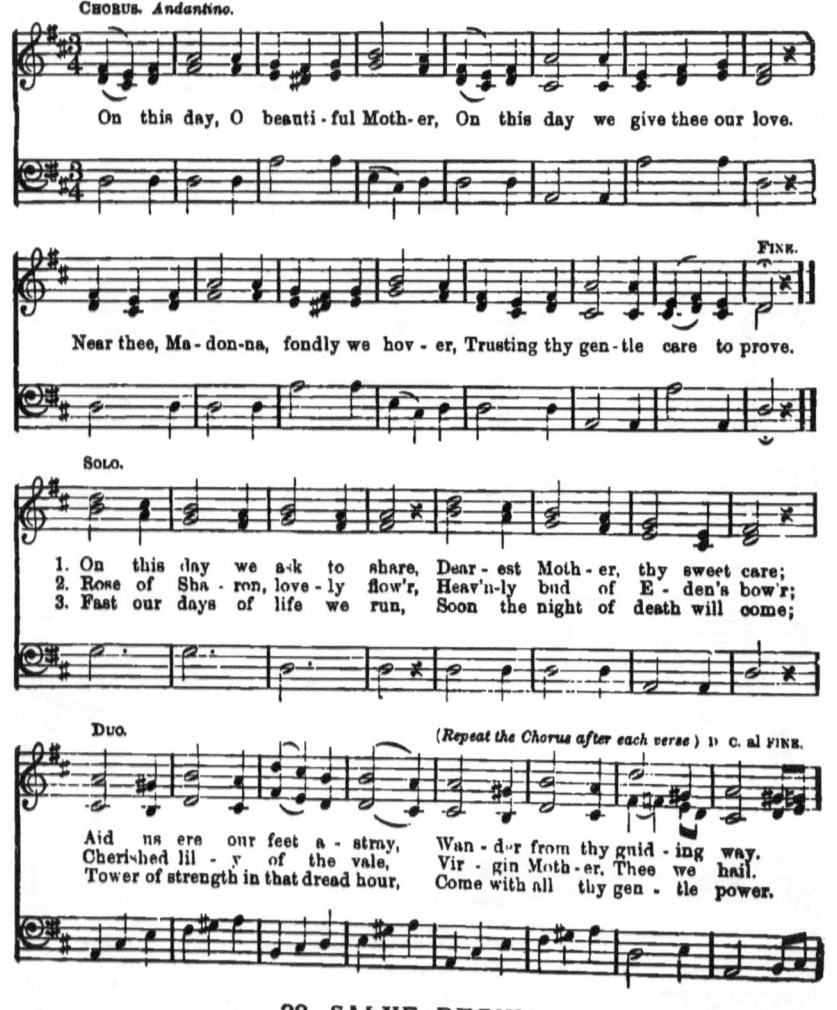

On this day, O beauti-ful Moth-er, On this day we give thee our love.

Near thee, Ma-don-na, fondly we hov-er, Trusting thy gen-tle care to prove.

1. On this day we ask to share, Dear-est Moth-er, thy sweet care;
2. Rose of Sha-ron, love-ly flow'r, Heav'n-ly bud of E-den's bow'r;
3. Fast our days of life we run, Soon the night of death will come;

Aid us ere our feet a-stray, Wan-der from thy guid-ing way.
Cherished lil-y of the vale, Vir-gin Moth-er, Thee we hail.
Tower of strength in that dread hour, Come with all thy gen-tle power.

22. SALVE REGINA.

(See page 35.)

23. THE MEMORARE.

CHORUS. *Allegretto.*

1. Oh! be thou mind-ful, Moth-er most ten-der, Ne'er was thine aid im-

plored in.... vain; Faint in the com-bat, lest we sur-ren-der, Do

FINE.

thou our fal-t'ring heart sus-tain, Do thou our fal-t'ring heart sus-tain.

DUO.

2. In a ges gone by, as all rec-ords de-clare, Not once hast thou
3. For this, in the midst of my sin and my dread, At the thought of thy
4. Though count-less and griev-ous the sins I de-plore, De-spair at thy
5. To my pray'rs and my sighs, bless-ed Moth-er, give ear, And be thou as

slight-ed the sup-pli-ant's cry; Nor shall a-ges that fol-low thy mer-cies im-
mer-cies with hope I'm in-spired; O ... Vir-gin! thy Son on the cross for me
name from my bo-som shall flee; In thy love will I hope for my par-don once
ev-er, the pen-i-tent's friend; 'Neath the shield of thy fa-vor no dan-ger I'll

Repeat Chorus after each verse.

pair; To all that in-voke thee, sweet Mother, thou'rt nigh, sweet Moth-er, thou'rt nigh.
bled: Thy Son on the cross for my ran-som ex-pired, for my ran-som ex-pired.
more, O Vir-gin and Moth-er, I fly un-to thee, I fly un-to thee.
fear, But with thee and thy Son hope to reign in the end, to reign in the end.

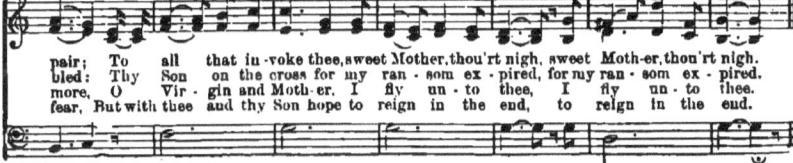

24. MOTHER DEAR.

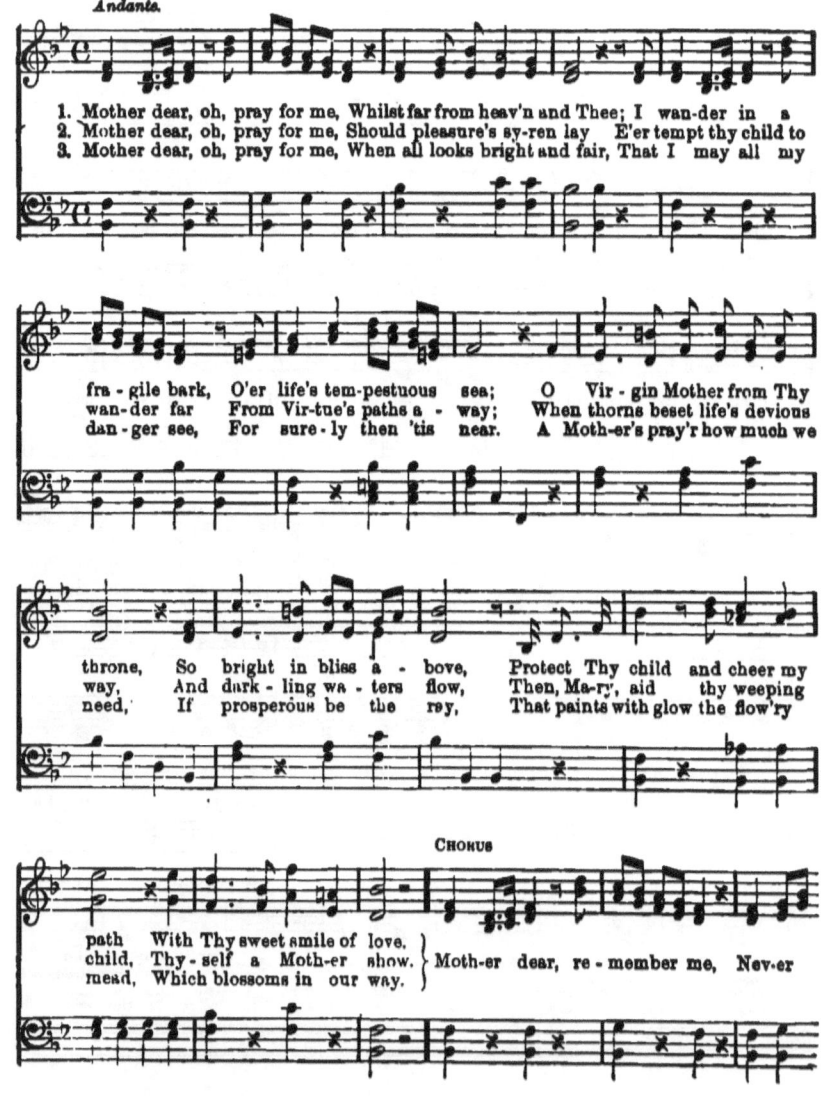

1. Mother dear, oh, pray for me, Whilst far from heav'n and Thee; I wan-der in a
2. Mother dear, oh, pray for me, Should pleasure's sy-ren lay   E'er tempt thy child to
3. Mother dear, oh, pray for me, When all looks bright and fair, That I   may all   my

fra - gile bark,   O'er life's tem-pestuous   sea;   O   Vir - gin Mother from Thy
wan-der far   From Vir-tue's paths a - way;   When thorns beset life's devious
dan - ger see,   For sure - ly then 'tis near.   A Moth-er's pray'r how much we

throne,   So   bright in bliss a - bove,   Protect Thy child and cheer my
way,   And dark - ling wa - ters   flow,   Then, Ma-ry', aid   thy weeping
need,   If   prosperous be   the   ray,   That paints with glow the flow'ry

CHORUS

path   With Thy sweet smile of love.)
child,   Thy - self a Moth-er show. } Moth-er dear, re - member me, Nev-er
mead,   Which blossoms in our way.)

MOTHER DEAR. Concluded.

cease Thy care, 'Till in heav'n e - ter - nal - ly Thy love and bliss I share.

25. HAIL, QUEEN OF HEAVEN.

Andante.

1. Hail, Queen of heav'n, the o - cean Star: Guide of the wand'rer here be - low,
2. O gen-tle, chaste, and spot-less Maid, We sinners make our prayers thro' thee;
3. So - journers in this vale of tears, To thee, blest Ad-vo - cate, we cry;
4. And while to Him who reigns a - bove In Godhead One, in Per - son Three,

Thrown on life's surge we claim thy care; Save us from per - il and from woe.
Re - mind thy Son that he has paid The price of our in - i - qui-ty,
Pit - y our sor - rows, calm our fears, And soothe with hope our mis-er - y.
The source of life, of grace, of love, Hom-age we pay on bend-ed knee;

Moth-er of Christ, Star of the sea, Pray for the wand'rer, pray for me.
Vir - gin most pure. Star of the sea, Pray for the sin - ner, pray for me.
Ref - uge in grief, Star of the sea, Pray for the mourner, pray for me.
Do thou, bright Queen, Star of the sea, Pray for thy children, pray for me.

26. SWEET MAY.

1. 'Tis the month of our Moth - er, The bless-ed and beau-ti - ful days,
2. Oh! what peace to her chil - dren, 'Mid sor- rows and tri - als to know,
3. And what joy to the err - ing, The sin - ful and sor - row-ful soul;
4. Let us sing then, re - joic - ing, That God hath so hon - or'd our race,

When our lips and our spir - its Are glowing with love and with praise.
That the love of their Moth - er Hath ev - er a so - lace for woe.
That a trust in her guid - ance Will lead to a glo - ri - ous goal.
As to clothe with our na - ture, Sweet Ma-ry the Moth-er of grace.

CHORUS.

All hail to dear Ma - ry! The guar- dian of our way,....

To the fair - est of Queens, Be the fair - est of seasons, sweet May.

27. REGINA CŒLI.
(See page 37.)

28. HAIL, MARY.

Andante con moto.

1. Hail! Ma - ry. Queen and Vir - gin pure, With ev - ery grace re - plete;
3. How oft, when trou - ble filled my breast, Or sin my conscience pained,

Hail! kind pro - tec - tress of the poor, Pit - y...... our need - y state.
Thro' thee, I sought for peace and rest, Thro' thee... I peace ob - tain'd.

2. O thou who fill'st the high - est place, Next heav'n's im - pe - rial throne,
4. Then, hence, in all my pains and cares, I'll seek for help in thee,

Ob - tain for us each sav - ing grace, And make our wants thine own.
E'er trust - ing thro' thy pow'r - ful pray'rs, To gain.... e - ter - ni - ty.

29. HOLY MARY, MOTHER MILD.

SOLO. *Allegretto.*   SEMI-CHORUS.

1. Ho - ly Ma - ry, Moth - er mild,
2. Who on life's tem - pes - tuous sea,
3. Waves of sor - row o'er me roll,
4. Dang-ers press on ev - ery side,
5. Brightest in the courts a - bove!
6. Com - fort of the sor-rowing, hear!

O sweet, sweet Mother!

SOLO.   SEMI-CHORUS.

1. Hear, O hear a fee - ble child,
2. Is cast a - lone: oh, succor me,
3. Storms of pas - sion shake my soul,
4. Star of o - cean, be my guide,
5. Joy of an - gels! Queen of love!
6. Grief and tears will dis - ap - pear,

O sweet, sweet Moth-er!

FULL CHORUS.

O, ex - ult, ye Cher - u - bim! And re-joice, ye Ser - a-phim!

Praise her! praise her! O praise our spot - less Queen!

30. BRIGHT QUEEN OF HEAVEN.

Cantabile.

1. Bright Queen of Heav - en, Vir - gin most fair,   Ma - ry most gen - tle,
3. Tho' night be lone - ly, Why should we fear,   While thy soft gleam - ing

1. List to our pray'r: Moth-er pro-tect us, Aid to us bring,   Sweetly en-
3. Shineth so near;   Lead-ing us gent - ly, 'Mid darkling gloom,   Beck'ning us

CHORUS.

1. fold us 'neath Thy shelt'ring wing. 2. Star of   the   o - cean,   Shed-ding soft
3. on - wards To our true home. 4. Soon may the   morrow,   Of bright end-less

2. light,   So - lace   in sor - row, Rest 'mid   the   night; Send, in our
4. day,   Chase the   drear vis-ions Of dark night a - way; Waft our lone

BRIGHT QUEEN OF HEAVEN. Concluded.

2. slumbers. Peace from a - bove, Shine on us ev - er, Bright Star of Love.
4. spir - its To Heav'n's bright shore, Where we may love thee, And rest e'er - more.

31. HOLY NAME OF JESUS.

f Andante.

1. { Je - sus, the ver - y thought of Thee, With sweetness fills my breast,
   But sweet-er far Thy face to see, And in Thy presence rest. }

CHORUS.

2. Nor voice can sing nor heart can frame A sweet - er sound than

Thy dear name; O Saviour of man-kind, O Sav-iour of man-kind.

Repeat the 2d verse after each of the following:

3. O hope of every contrite heart,
    O joy of all the meek,
To those who fall how kind Thou art!
    How good to those who seek !

4. But what to those who find ? ah ! this
    Nor tongue nor pen can show:

The love of Jesus, what it is,
    None but His loved ones know.

5. Jesus ! our only joy be Thou,
    As Thou our prize wilt be :
Jesus ! be Thou our glory now,
    And through eternity !

32. THE HEART OF JESUS.

1. O sa - cred Heart! with burn - ing love On Thee en -
2. Thou, Heart of Je - sus! art the throne Of mer - cy,
3. O Lamb of God! meek vic - tim, slain For us, let
4. God's Moth - er! Vir - gin ev - er blest! Thy heart and

rapt - ured an - gels gaze; To Thee tri - umph - ant Saints a -
Thou the fount of grace; Our hope of heav'n from Thee a -
not the stream that flowed From Thy pierc'd Heart have flowed in
His are al - ways one; Plead thou our cause; thy sweet re -

bove For - ev - er sing their grate - ful praise.
lone, Sole ref - uge of our fall - en race.
vain, Oh! cleanse us with Thy pre - cious blood.
quest Is nev - er slight - ed by thy Son.

Chorus.

O sa - cred Heart may we a - dore, And love Thee ev - er more and more.

33. TO JESUS' HEART.

1. To Je - sus' Heart, all burn - ing, With fer - vent love for men, My
2. O Heart for me on fire........ With love no man can speak, My
3. Too true, I have for - sak - en Thy flock, by wil - ful sin; Yet
4. As Thou art meek and low - ly, And ev - er pure of heart, So
5. When life a - way is fly - ing, And earth's false glare is done, Still

heart with fond - est yearn - ing Shall raise the joy - ful strain.
yet un - told de - sire........ God gives me for Thy sake.
now let me be ta - ken Back to Thy fold a - gain.
may my heart be whol - ly, Of Thine the coun - ter - part.
sa - cred Heart, in dy - ing, I'll say I'm all Thine own.

Chorus.

While a - ges course a - long, Blest be with loud - est song The

sa - cred Heart of Je - sus, By ev - ery heart and tongue, The

TO JESUS' HEART. Concluded.

sa - cred Heart of Je - sus, By ev - ery heart and tongue.

34. JESUS IN THE BLESSED SACRAMENT.

SOLO. *Andante.*

1. My God, my Life, my Love........ To Thee, to Thee I
2. My faith be - holds Thee, Lord!...... Con - cealed in hu - man
3. Oh! when wilt Thou be min·,....... Sweet lov - er of my
4. Oh! come and fix Thy thron·,...... With - in my ver - y
5. Be - gone ye, from my 'mind,....... Vain, child - ish, earth - ly

DUO.

call:........ O come to me from heav'n a - bove, And
food;....... My sens - es fail, but in Thy word I
soul?....... My Je - sus dear, my King di - vine, Come
heart,....... Oh! make it burn for Thee a - lone, And
toys!.... .. In Je - sus on - ly do I find True

CHOR.

be by God, my all,.... And be my God, my all........
trust, and find my God,... I trust, and find my God........
o'er my heart to rule,... Come o'er my heart to rule........
from me ne'er de - part,... And from me ne'er de - part.......
pleas - ures, sol - id joys,... True pleas-ures, sol - id joys........

35. ADORO TE.

Adagio.

1. A - do - ro te de - vo - te, la - tens De - i - tas,
    Ti - bi se cor me - um to - tum sub - ji - cit,
2. O me - mo - ri - al - e mor - tis Do - mi - ni,
    Præ - sta me - æ men - ti de te vi - ve - re,
3. Je - su, quem ve - la - . tum nunc as - pi - ci - o.
    Ut te re - ve - la - ta cer - nens fa - ci - - e,

1. Quæ sub his fi - gu - ris ve - re la - ti - tas;
    Qui - a te con - tem - plans to - tum de - fi - cit.
2. Pa - nis vi - vus vi - tam præs - tans ho - mi - ni,
    Et te il - li sem - per dul - ce sa - po - re,
3. O - ro fi - at il - lud quod tam si - ti - o,
    Vi - su sim be - a - tus tu - æ glo - ri - æ.

f A - ve Je - su ve - rum man - hu, Christe Je - su!

p Ad - au - ge fi - dem o - mni - um in te cre - den - ti - um.

36. VENI JESU.

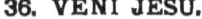

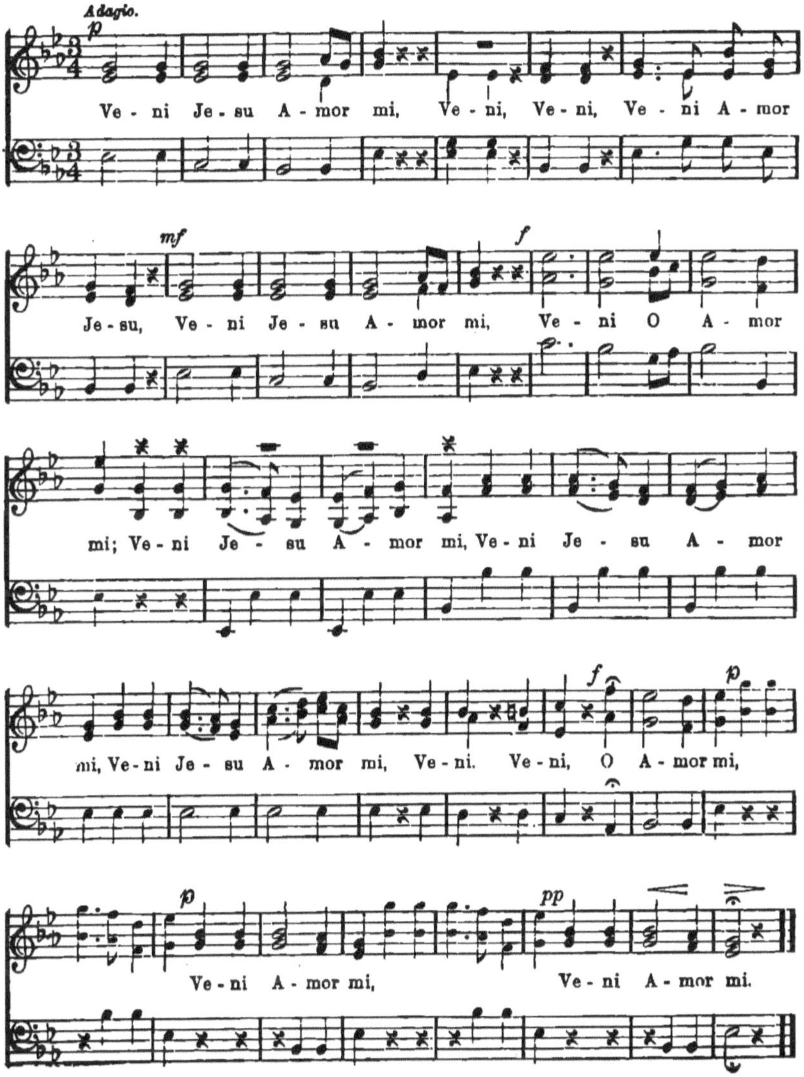
Adagio.
p
Ve - ni Je - su A - mor mi, Ve - ni, Ve - ni, Ve - ni A - mor
mf
f
Je - su, Ve - ni Je - su A - mor mi, Ve - ni O A - mor
mi; Ve - ni Je - su A - mor mi, Ve - ni Je - su A - mor
f
p
mi, Ve - ni Je - su A - mor mi, Ve - ni. Ve - ni, O A - mor mi,
p
pp
Ve - ni A - mor mi, Ve - ni A - mor mi.

37. JESU DULCIS MEMORIA.

Andante.

1. Je - su! dul - cis me - mo - ri - a, Dans ver - a cor - dis
2. Nil ca - ni - tur su - a - vi - us, Au - di - tur nil ju -
3. Je - su, spes pœ - ui - ten - ti - bus, Quam pi - us es pe -

gau - di - a; Sed su - per mel et om - ni - a, E - jus dul -
cun - di - us, Nil co - gi - ta - tur dul - ci - us, Quam Je - su
ten - ti - bus, Quam bo - nus te quæ - ren - ti - bus! Sed quid in -

cis præ - sen - ti - a.
De - i Fi - li - us. } Je - su, Je - su, dul - cis me - mo - ri - a.
ve - ni - en - ti - bus.

38. ACTS OF FAITH, DESIRE, Etc.

Andante.

1. In this Sa - cra - ment, sweet Je - sus, Thou dost give Thy flesh and blood,
2. Yes, dear Je - sus, I be - lieve it, And Thy pres - ence I a - dore,
3. Come, sweet Je - sus, in Thy mer - cy, Give Thy flesh and blood to me;
4. Come, that I may live for - ev - er, Thou in me, and I in Thee;

With Thy soul and God - head al - so, As our own most pre - cious food.
And with all my heart I love Thee, May I love Thee more and more.
Come to me. O dear - est Je - sus, Come, my soul's true life to be.
Liv - ing thus I shall not per - ish, But shall live e - ter - nal - ly.

39. JESUS, SAVIOUR OF MY SOUL.

1. Je - sus, Sav - iour of my soul, Let me to Thy ref - uge fly,
2. Oth - er re - fuge have I none: Hangs my help - less soul on Thee,

While the near - er wa - ters roll, While the tem - pest still is nigh;
Leave, ah, leave me not a - lone, Still sup - port and com - fort me;

Hide me, O my Sav - iour, hide, Till the storm of life is past:
All my trust on Thee is stay'd, All my help from Thee I bring;

Safe in - to Thy ha - ven guide, O re - ceive my soul at last.
Cov - er my de - fence-less head With the shad - ow of Thy wing.

40. WHAT HAPPINESS CAN EQUAL MINE?

1. What hap - pi - ness can e - qual mine? I've found the ob - ject of my love:
3. My Love is mine, and I am His; In me He dwells, in Him I live;
5. Dear Je - sus, now my heart is Thine, Oh, may it nev - er from Thee fly;

My Sav - iour and my Lord di - vine Is come to me from heav'n a - bove.
Where could I taste a pur - er bliss? What greater boon could Je - sus give?
My God, be Thou for - ev - er mine, And I Thine own e - ter - nal - ly.

TRIO.

2. He makes my heart His own a - bode; His flesh be - comes my dai - ly bread;
4. O roy - al banquet! heav'n-ly feast; O flow - ing Fount of life and grace!
6. No more, O Sa - tan, thee I fear! O world, thy charms I now de - spise;

CHORUS.

He pours on me His heal-ing blood; And with His life my soul is fed.
Where the God giv - er, man the gue-t, Meet and u - nite in sweet em - brace.
For Christ Him-self is with me here, My joy, my life, my par - a - dise!

41. TE DEUM LAUDAMUS.

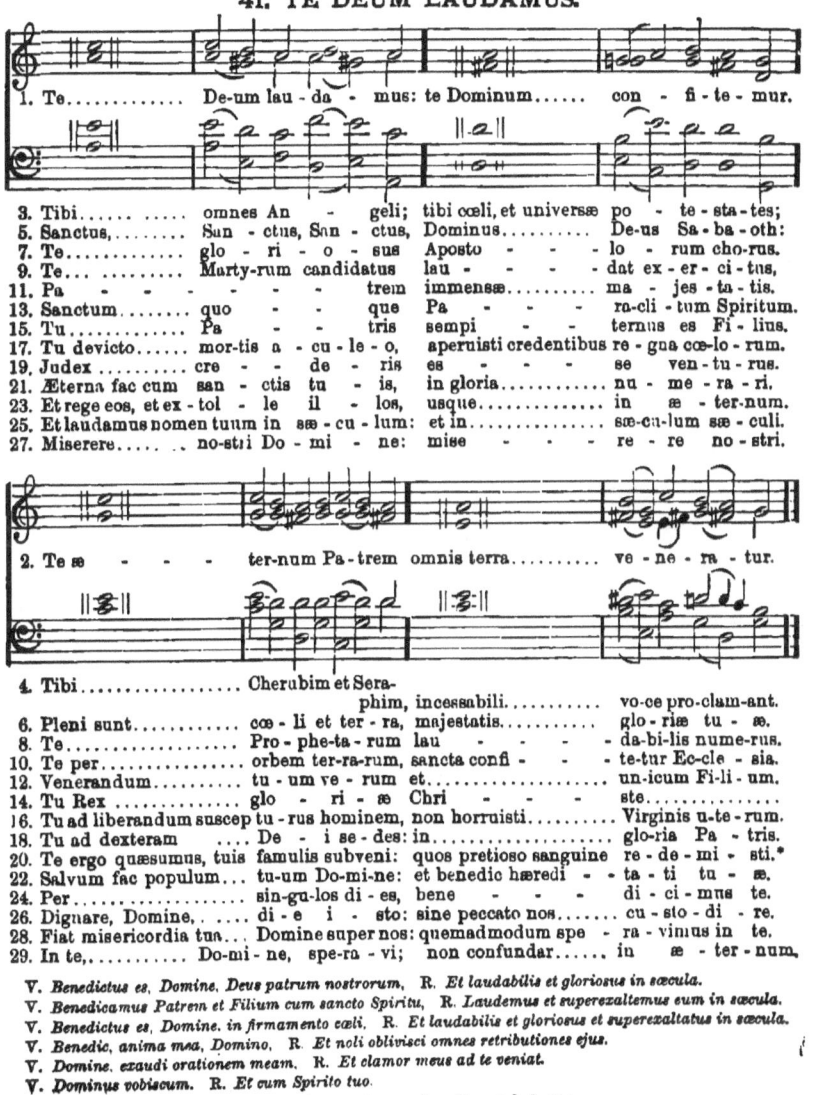

1. Te............ De-um lau - da - mus: te Dominum...... con - fi - te - mur.

3. Tibi..........	omnes An - geli;	tibi cœli, et universæ po - te - sta - tes;
5. Sanctus,........	San - ctus, San - ctus,	Dominus......... De-us Sa - ba - oth:
7. Te............	glo - ri - o - sus	Aposto - - - lo - rum cho-rus.
9. Te............	Marty-rum candidatus	lau - - - - dat ex - er - ci - tus,
11. Pa - - - - - -	trem	immensæ.......... ma - jes - ta - tis.
13. Sanctum........	quo - - que	Pa - - - ra-cli - tum Spiritum.
15. Tu............	Pa - - tris	sempi - - ternus es Fi - lius.
17. Tu devicto......	mor-tis a - cu - le - o,	aperuisti credentibus re - gna cœ-lo - rum.
19. Judex..........	cre - - de - ris	es - - - se ven - tu - rus.
21. Æterna fac cum	san - ctis tu - is,	in gloria............ nu - me - ra - ri.
23. Et rege eos, et ex - tol - le il - los,		usque.............. in æ - ter-num.
25. Et laudamus nomen tuum in sæ - cu - lum:		et in.............. sæ-cu-lum sæ - culi.
27. Miserere........ no-stri Do - mi - ne:		mise - - - re - re no - stri.

2. Te æ - - - - ter-num Pa - trem omnis terra.......... ve - ne - ra - tur.

4. Tibi................	Cherubim et Sera- phim, incessabili..........	vo-ce pro-clam-ant.
6. Pleni sunt............	cœ - li et ter - ra, majestatis..........	glo - riæ tu - æ.
8. Te..................	Pro - phe-ta - rum lau - - -	- da-bi-lis nume-rus.
10. Te per...............	orbem ter-ra-rum, sancta confi -	- te-tur Ec-cle - sia.
12. Venerandum..........	tu - um ve - rum et..............	un-icum Fi-li - um.
14. Tu Rex..............	glo - ri - æ Chri - - -	ste..............
16. Tu ad liberandum suscep tu - rus hominem, non horruisti..........		Virginis u-te - rum.
18. Tu ad dexteram .... De - i se - des: in..........		glo-ria Pa - tris.
20. Te ergo quæsumus, tuis famulis subveni: quos pretioso sanguine re - de - mi - sti.*		
22. Salvum fac populum... tu-um Do-mi-ne: et benedic hæredi - - ta - ti tu - æ.		
24. Per.................. sin-gu-los di - es, bene - - - di - ci - mus te.		
26. Dignare, Domine,. .... di - e i - sto: sine peccato nos....... cu - sto - di - re.		
28. Fiat misericordia tua... Domine super nos: quemadmodum spe - ra - vimus in te.		
29. In te,.......... Do-mi - ne, spe-ra - vi; non confundar...... in æ - ter - num.		

V. *Benedictus es, Domine. Deus patrum nostrorum,* R. *Et laudabilis et gloriosus in sæcula.*
V. *Benedicamus Patrem et Filium cum sancto Spiritu,* R. *Laudemus et superexaltemus eum in sæcula.*
V. *Benedictus es, Domine. in firmamento cæli,* R. *Et laudabilis et gloriosus et superexaltatus in sæcula.*
V. *Benedic, anima mea, Domino,* R. *Et noli oblivisci omnes retributiones ejus.*
V. *Domine. exaudi orationem meam,* R. *Et clamor meus ad te veniat.*
V. *Dominus vobiscum.* R. *Et cum Spirito tuo.*

* The 20th verse is sung kneeling and slowly.

42. ST. PATRICK.*

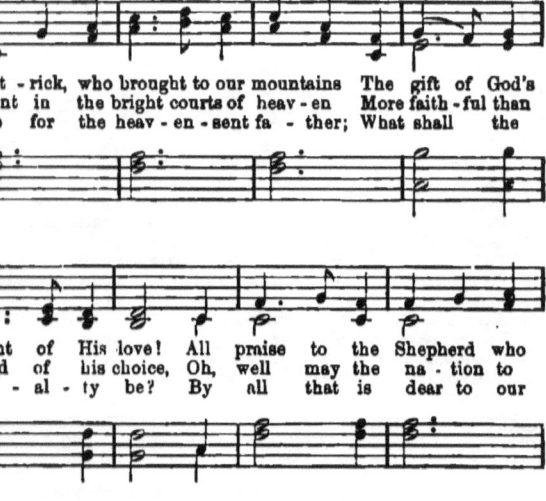

mf Andantino.

1. All praise to St. Pat - rick, who brought to our mountains The gift of God's
2. There is not a saint in the bright courts of heav - en More faith - ful than
3. Then what shall we do for the heav - en - sent fa - ther; What shall the

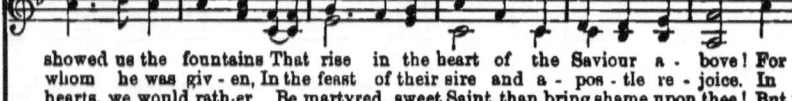

faith, the sweet light of His love! All praise to the Shepherd who
he to the land of his choice, Oh, well may the na - tion to
proof of our loy - al - ty be? By all that is dear to our

showed us the fountains That rise in the heart of the Saviour a - bove! For
whom he was giv - en, In the feast of their sire and a - pos - tle re - joice. In
hearts, we would rath-er Be martyred, sweet Saint, than bring shame upon thee! But

hundreds of years, In smiles and in tears, Our Saint hath been with us, our
glo - ry a - bove, And true to his love, He keeps the false faith from his
oh, he will take The prom-ise we make, So to live that our lives, by God's

* Great care must be taken not to sing the above hymn too quickly, as its beauty is frequently not
only marred but utterly destroyed by this fault.

ST. PATRICK. Concluded.

shield and our stay! All else may have gone—St. Pat - rick a - lone— He
chil - dren a - way, And the dark false faith— Is far worse than death— Oh,
help may dis - play The light that he bore To Er - in's green shore. Yes!

hath been to us light, when earth's lights were all set, For the glo - ries of
he drives it far off from the green sun - ny shore, Like the rep - tiles which
Fa - ther of Ire - land! no child wilt thou own, Whose life is not

faith they can nev - er de - cay, And the best of 'our glo - ries is
fled from his curse in dis - may, And Er - in when Er - ror's proud
light - ed by grace on its way; For they are true I - rish, ah,

bright with us yet, In the faith and the feast of St. Pat - rick's day.
tri - umph is o - ver, Will still be found keep- ing St. Pat - rick's day.
yes, they a - lone, Whose hearts are all true on St. Pat - rick's day.

43. HOLY GOD.

44. FADING, STILL FADING.

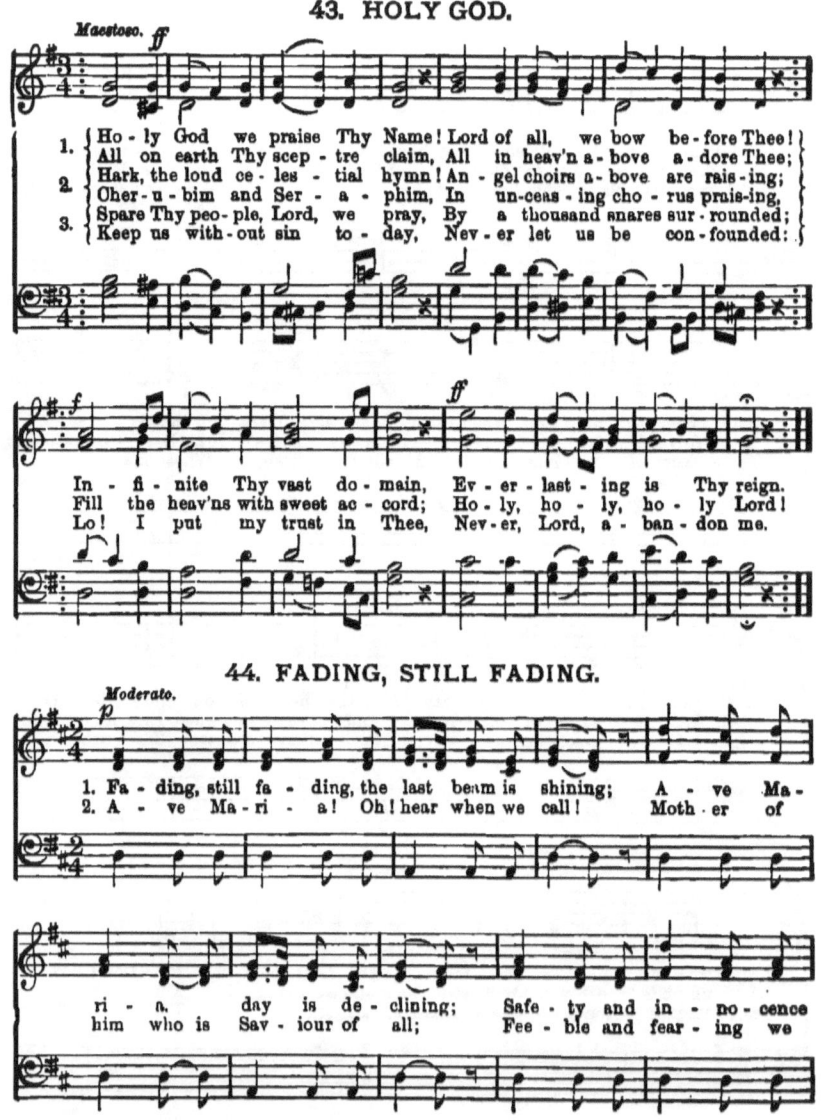

FADING, STILL FADING. Concluded.

fly with the light, Tempta - tion and dan - ger walk forth in the
trust in thy might, In doubt-ing and dark - ness, thy love be our

night; From the fall of the shade till the ma - tin shall chime; —
light; Let us sleep on thy breast while the night-ta - per burns, And

CHORUS.

Shield us from dan - ger and save us from crime. } A - ve Ma - ri - a,
wake in thine arms when the morn-ing re - turns. }

A - ve Ma - ri - a, A - ve Ma - ri - a, au - - di nos.

45. JERUSALEM, MY HAPPY HOME.

1. Je - ru - sa - lem, my hap - py home, How do I sigh for
2. No sun, no moon in bor-rowed light Re - volves thine hours a-
3. From ev - ery eye He wipes the tear, All sighs and sor - rows
4. The thought of thee to us is giv'n, Our sor - rows to be -

thee! When shall my ex - ile have an end, Thy joys when
way; The Lamb on Cal - v'ry's mount-ain slain Is thy e -
cease; No more al - ter - nate hope and fear, But ev - er -
guile, To an - ti - ci - pate the bliss of Heav'n, In His e -

shall I see?
ter - nal day.
last - ing peace.
ter - nal smile.

CHORUS.

Je - ru - sa - lem, Je - ru - sa - lem, Je -

ru - sa - lem, my hap - py home, How do I sigh for thee!

46. THE GUARDIAN ANGEL.

1. Dear An-gel ev-er at my side, How lov-ing must thou be; To leave thy home in heav'n to guide A lit-tle child like me,............ A lit-tle child like me.

2. Thy beau-ti-ful and shin-ing face I see not, though so near; The sweet-ness of thy soft low voice I am too deaf to hear,.......... I am too deaf to hear:

3. I can-not feel thee touch my hand With pres-sure light and mild, To check me as my moth-er did When I was but a child,.......... When I was but a child.

4. But I have felt thee in my thoughts,
Fighting with sin for me;
And when my heart loves God, I know
‖: The sweetness is from thee. :‖

5. And when, dear Spirit! I kneel down
Morning and night to prayer,
Something there is within my heart
‖: That tells me thou art there. :‖

6. Then for thy sake, dear Angel! now
More humble will I be;
But I am weak, and when I fall,
‖: Oh, weary not of me. :‖

7. Oh, weary not, but love me still,
For Mary's sake, thy Queen;
She never tired of me, though I
‖: Her worst of sons have been. :‖

8. She will reward thee with a smile;
Thou know'st what it is worth!
For Mary's smiles each day convert
‖: The hardest hearts on earth. :‖

9. Then love me, love me, Angel dear!
And I will love thee more;
And help me when my soul is cast
‖: Upon the eternal shore. :‖

Requiem Mass

Re - qui - em æ - ter - nam do - na e - is, Do - - mi-ne et lux per-pe-tu-a lu - ce-at e - - is.

(Ps) Te de - cet hymnus Deus in.... Si - on et ti - bi reddetur votum in Je - ru - sa - lem:

Repeat Requiem, etc., as far as *Te decet*.

e - xau - di orationem meam,.......... ad te omnis.......... ca - ro ve - ni-et.

KYRIE. Repeat each three times.

Ky - ri-e e - lei - son, Ky-ri - e e - - - - le - i - son.
Chri - - ste e - lei - son,

V. *Dominus vobiscum.* R. *Et cum spiritu tuo.*
V. *Oremus........* R. *Amen.*

SEQUENCE.

1. Di - es i - ræ, di - es il - la, Sol - vet sæ - clum in fa - vil - la:
2. Quantus tre-mor est fu - tu - rus, Quan - do Ju - dex est ven - tu - rus,

OFFERTORY.

Do - mi - ne Je - su Chri - ste, Rex.......... glo - - - - - ri - æ,

li - be - ra a - ni - mas o - mni - um fi - de - li - um de - fun - cto - rum

de pœ - nis in - fer - ni, et de pro - fun - do la - cu: li - be - ra

e - as de o - - - - re le - o - - nis, ne ab - sor - be - at e - as

tar - - ta - rus, ne ca - dant in ob - scu - - rum, sed si - gni - fer

san - ctus Mi - cha - el re - præ - sen - tet e - - as in lu - cam

V. *Per omnia sæcula sæculorum.* R. *Amen.*
V. *Dominus vobiscum.* R. *Et cum spiritu tuo.*
V. *Sursum Corda.* R. *Habemus ad Dominum.*
V. *Gratias, etc.* R. *Dignum et justum est.* V. *Vere, etc.*

SANCTUS.

V. *Per omnia sæcula sæculorum.* R. *Amen.*
After the Pater noster. R. *Sed libera nos a malo.*
V. *Per omnia, etc.* R. *Amen*
V. *Pax Domini sit semper vobiscum.* R. *Et cum spiritu tuo.*

AGNUS DEI.   Three times.   I & 2 time. | 3d time.

COMMUNION.

V. *Dominus vobiscum.* R. *Et cum spiritu tuo.*
V. *Oremus, etc.* R. *Amen.*
V. *Dominus vobiscum.* R. *Et cum spiritu tuo.*
V. *Requiescat in pace.* R. *Amen.*

LIBERA.

V. Tremens fa·ctus·sum e·go et ti — me·o, dum dis·cus·si·o ve — ne·rit,

(Return to ✱, and repeat *Quando*)
(*cœli*, etc., as far as "*terra*" incl.)

at·que ven·tu·ra i·ra. V. Di·es il·la, di·es i·ræ, ca·la·mi·ta·tis...

(Return to ✱✱, and repeat *Dum veneris*,)
etc., as far as "*per ignem*" inclusive.)

et mi·se·ri·æ, di·es mag·na et a·ma·ra.. val·de. V. Re·qui·em æ·ter·nam

Repeat *Libera* as far as "*Tremens.*"

do·na e·.is, Do — mi·ne, et lux per·pe·tu·a lu·ce·at e·is.

The "Libera" ended, one or a few singers chant: Ky·ri·e e·lo·i·son.
The choir responds: Chri·ste e·le·i·son.

Then all together chant: Ky·ri·e e — le·i·son.

V. *Pater noster* (the rest being said in silence).
V. *Et ne nos inducas in tentationem.* R. *Sed libera nos a malo.*
V. *A porta inferi.* R. *Erue, Domine, animam ejus.*
V. *Requiescat in pace.* R. *Amen.*
V. *Domine exaudi orationem meam.* R. *Et clamor meus ad te veniat.*
V. *Dominus vobiscum.* R. *Et cum spiritu tuo.*
V. *Oremus*, etc. R. *Amen.*
V. *Requiem æternam dona ei, Domine.* R. *Et lux perpetua luceat ei.*
V. *Requiescat in pace.* R. *Amen.*